I0649162

George Outram

Legal and Other Lyrics

With Explantory Notes and a Glossary

George Outram

Legal and Other Lyrics
With Explantory Notes and a Glossary

ISBN/EAN: 9783744782333

Printed in Europe, USA, Canada, Australia, Japan

Cover: Foto ©Andreas Hilbeck / pixelio.de

More available books at **www.hansebooks.com**

LEGAL AND OTHER LYRICS

BY THE LATE

GEORGE OUTRAM

*A NEW EDITION, WITH EXPLANATORY NOTES
AND A GLOSSARY*

EDITED BY

J. H. STODDART, LL.D.

AND ILLUSTRATED BY

WILLIAM RALSTON AND A. S. BOYD

WILLIAM BLACKWOOD AND SONS
EDINBURGH AND LONDON
MDCCCLXXXVIII

PREFACE.

THE demand for the 'Legal Lyrics' of George
Outram, when the volume was published
some years ago, was, after a second edition,
greater than the supply, although several
thousand copies were sold. The volume is
now out of print, and commands a considerable price in the book market when a copy
is exposed at auction. The representatives
of the family of Mr Outram have now
thought the time has come for the publication of a new edition, with several emenda-
tions upon the text of the last, which was
not quite according to the original. The
editor has adhered as closely as possible to

the original verses, only making some very
slight alterations that seemed necessary for
the present time. He has also, after a close
examination of the other poems of Mr Outram, added a few pieces not before published,
but which seemed to him characteristic of the
genius of the author. He might have given
many other pieces of Mr Outram's, that forty
years ago would have taken a good place in
literature; but George Outram, unfortunately
for his own reputation, wrote only for his
friends, and not for posterity, and was willing to allow his more sober and elevating
poems to lie aside. The illustrations by Mr
Ralston and Mr Boyd, it may be hoped, will
give additional interest to the little volume
that the editor now presents as the complete
poetical works of one of the most genial and
humorous of Scotchmen. The interesting
notes to "The Faculty Roll" and other legal
songs are supplied by an old and intimate
friend of Mr Outram, who had the merit of
extracting from him one evening, after a day's
fishing on the Tweed, the song of "The

Saumon," and also, from time to time, a good
many stanzas of "The Annuity," which Mr
Outram sent him, to be sung at the annual
dinner of a life insurance association with
which he was connected, and at which "The
Annuity" was always called for. It may be
also necessary to remark that the poems, as
the judicious reader will readily perceive, are
purely dramatic, and that the author ex-
presses not his own experiences, but those
of the type most familiar in Scottish society
in his day. George Outram himself was the
most refined, gentle, and humane man of his
time.

J. H. S.

LEDDRIEGREEN,

March 1887.

CONTENTS.

—

CONTENTS.

LIST OF ILLUSTRATIONS.

INTRODUCTORY NOTICE

INTRODUCTORY NOTICE TO FIRST EDITION.

By the late HENRY GLASSFORD BELL, Esq.,
SHERIFF OF LANARKSHIRE.

GEORGE OUTRAM was born on the 25th March 1805, at Clyde Iron-Works, in the vicinity of Glasgow, his father being then the manager of these important works. In the course of a year or two, however, the family removed from Glasgow to Leith, Mr Outram, sen., having become partner in a mercantile house there. George received his early education in the High School of Leith ; and afterwards went through the regular curriculum of the University of Edinburgh. In 1827 he became a member of the Faculty of Advocates, and for the next ten years continued to attend the Parliament House, where his genial disposition and fund of quaint humour made him a great favourite with both Bench and Bar.

Being, however, of a retiring, sensitive, and not

A

over-active nature, Outram did not lay himself out
with much earnestness for legal practice; and in
1837 he accepted the offer, somewhat unexpectedly
made to him, of the editorship of the 'Glasgow
Herald,' then, as it has since continued to be, the
leading newspaper in the west of Scotland. He
became also one of the proprietors, and settled
down to his new duties for life. The 'Herald,' at
that time, was published only twice a-week, and
was conducted in a steady, quiet, and unpretentious
manner, with a careful avoidance of anything like
an aggressive or innovating spirit. In politics it
was mildly Conservative, but by no means slav-
ishly so, as it rather piqued itself on maintaining
a character of independence, and was on the whole
conducted with such tact and discrimination that
it secured the confidence of the public, and increased in circulation and repute. Its editor loved
what was old and pleasant and easy, and shrank,
with a sort of humorous abhorrence, from what was
novel and obtrusive, either in social or political life.
Nevertheless, when occasion required, he showed
both firmness and discrimination, and his judgment was seldom at fault in the numerous questions which force themselves on the attention of a
public writer.

Mr Outram had married before he left Edinburgh, and in due course became the father of four sons, in whose education and upbringing he took the greatest possible interest, but one of whom only now survives.* He had one daughter, who died in infancy. He resided, with much domestic enjoyment, in Glasgow or its neighbourhood for nineteen years. During that period he won and retained, by his amiable manners and delightful flow of good-natured humour, the esteem and respect of all classes. He likewise experienced much pleasure in keeping up his acquaintance with his old friends and associates in Edinburgh, who had greatly regretted his separation from them, and were always glad to receive him with open arms.

Latterly his constitution, which had never been very robust, gave way somewhat prematurely, and he died at his country residence of Rosemore, on the Holy Loch, on 15th September 1856, in the fifty-second year of his age. He was buried in Warriston Cemetery, Edinburgh; and left behind him, in the hearts of many attached friends, the memory of a most kindly, amiable, and gifted man.

* He has now 1887 been dead several years.

For George Outram possessed, in addition to his other qualifications, a spark of true and original Scottish genius, but for which the foregoing brief summary of his uneventful life would never have seen the light. This genius manifested itself chiefly in the production of songs and other lyrical pieces, mostly in the Scottish dialect, and exhibiting, without a touch of bitterness, an amount of humour hardly surpassed by any other national writer. Many of these compositions, which were the delight of his own circle, were called forth only by some incident or event in the lives of some of the members of that circle; so that their allusions and mirth-exciting power could not be rightly understood by the outer world. Well, however, do Outram's surviving friends remember what additional delight many a song of his, composed for the occasion, gave to their social symposiums. The author himself was of too modest a nature to regard them as anything but trifles; but when a copy was obtained, the unrepressed laughter of many a coterie in the Parliament House, collected in some convenient nook, indicated their appreciation of the contents.

Fortunately, however, some of Outram's best things are of a more general character, which appeal to, and are sure to command, the sympathies of all. His legal lyrics introduce us to some of the peculiarities of Scotch law, and show us their comic side with a rare and genial power, scarcely ever attempted before, and certainly never at any time surpassed. The author's idea in such ballads as "The Annuity," "The Multiplepoinding," "Soumin an' Roumin," "The Process of Augmentation," "The Process of Wakenin," "Cessio Bonorum," and others, seems to have been to present vivid and humorous pictures, not unaccompanied sometimes by a touch of pathos, of the peculiar and rather remarkable features of Scotch legal process, and its effect on the character and feelings of his countrymen. The scenes suggested are as vividly portrayed as they could have been by the pencil of a Wilkie; and whilst perhaps they will be most intensely appreciated by professional lawyers, they possess that breadth of colouring and truth to human nature which cannot fail to interest all readers, and entertain them with an exquisite perception of the ludicrous.

Some of the miscellaneous pieces are not less stamped with originality and humour, and it is much to be regretted that, for the reasons above indicated, they cannot be all given to the public.

It is confidently believed, however, that among the poems in the present publication there will be found specimens of national *facetiæ* differing from anything to be found elsewhere, and full of a high merit of their own. In some instances they are descriptive of bacchanalian characters; but, in place of being written with any view to encourage bacchanalian habits, they tend to expose the folly of such habits, and to turn them into ridicule. Here and there the author's keen sense of the ludicrous has induced a certain freedom of expression, without which the thought would have lost its characteristic vigour. But the consciousness of a healthy moral tone remains throughout.

This brief Introductory Notice ought perhaps to stop here. But it has been suggested that one or two personal reminiscences of Outram may be added, as tending to bring out more fully the genial character of the man and the poet. His cast of mind and associations were essentially Scottish. He was, it is believed, only twice out of Scotland during his life, and that but for short periods. He was admirably versed in, and had a high appreciation of, the strength of his native Doric. He was also familiar with the peculiarities of Scotch character, some of which afforded him great amusement, whilst others inspired him with respect. These features of his mind and habits led him, not long after he went to reside in Glasgow, to conceive the idea of a "Scotch Denner." to be given in his own house, as a purely national meal, to which each guest was to come in the costume of some favourite Scottish worthy, and which was to be a gathering ironically renewing the once popular lamentations over the Union with England, as destructive of the independence and ancient position of Scotland. The "denner," to which only a small and select party was invited, each of whom appeared in an historical character and dress, came off on 22d July 1844, being the 138th anniversary of the Treaty of Union. It had been a great amusement to Outram, in his leisure moments, to make arrangements for this banquet. He printed his letter of invitation—of itself a curiosity—a list of toasts—and, by way of *menu*, a small *brochure*, a copy of which was supplied to each of the guests, with the motto, "Syne there were proper stewards, cunning baxters, excellent cooks and potingars, with confections and drugs for their deserts."—Pitscottie, Edin. 1728, p. 174. The Letter of Invitation,

List of Toasts, and the *Brochure*, are here given
for the perusal of those who may be interested by
a specimen of the genial humour which habitually
pervaded the author's social intercourse with his
friends.

INVITATION.

———

"RICHT TRUSTIE FREEND,—

"Forgie me that I steer your memorie
e'en now, anent that wearifu' Treaty o' Union wi' the
Englishers, whilk, as ye weel ken, was subscrivit by
the unworthie representatives of our forebears, on the
22d day of July, A.D. 1706, in ane unhappie hour.
For I do sae allenarlie wi' the intent that ye suld
devise means to red us for aye of that wanchancie
covenant, the endurance whereof is regarded by ilka
leal-hearted Caledonian with never-devallin' scunner.
Wherefor I earnestly entreat of you that, on Monday
the 22d of the present month, bein' the 138th anniversary of the foresaid dulefu' event, ye wald attend
a great gatherin' o' Scotsmen, to be halden after the
gude auld Scottish fashion, at Scott Street of Glasgow, whan it will be taen into cannie consideration
how we may now best free oursels o' that unnatural
band, either by a backspang, if we can sae far be-

gunk the Southron, or by an evendown cassin o' the bargain, an' haudin' of our ain by the strong hand, if need be. An' to the intent that we may be the better preparit for what may come, it is designit, on the occasion of the said gatherin', that we sall subsist upon our ain national vivers allenarlie, an' sae pruive how far we can foregae the aids o' foreign countries in respect of our creature comforts, varyin' our fare wi' the flesh o' the red deer an' the trouts o' Lochleven, suppin' our ain Kail, Hotch Potch, or Cockieleekie, whiles pangin' oursels wi' haggis an' brose, an' whiles wi' sheep's head an' partan pies, rizzard haddies, crappit heads an' scate - rumples, nowt's feet, kebbucks, scadlips, an' skink, forbye custocks, carlings, rifarts an' syboes, farles, fadges an' ban- nocks, drammock, brochan an' powsowdie, and sik- like—washin' the same doun our craigs wi' nae foreign pushion, but allenarlie wi' our ain reamin' yill an' bellin' usquebaugh.

"Trustin' that you, an' mony anither leal Scotsman, will forgather at the foresaid time an' place, to bend the bicker after the manner of our worthie forebears when guid auld Scotland was a kingdom,

"I subscrieve myself,

"Yours to command,

"GEORGE OUTRAM.

"Given at Scott Street of Glasgow, on the eleventh day o' July, Anno Domini, mdcccxliv."

On the back of the letter, under the address, were the words :—

" Be this letter delivered with haste—haste—post
haste !
Ride, villain, ride !
For thy life—for thy life—for thy life !"

The late Lord Cockburn threatened to interdict
the treasonable meeting! But the guests, nevertheless, assembled, and found prepared for them
the following bill of fare :—

"Ane Buik o' Ancient Scotch Dishes for the Gatherin'."

TABLE I.

(1) "*There's peas intil't, an' there's beans intil't,*
An' there's carrots, an' neeps, an' greens intil't."

—o—

(2) "*Lang may she live, an' lang enjoy*
Ilk blessin' life can gie,—
Health, wealth, content, an' pleasour,
An' cockie-leekie."

TABLE II.

(3) "*Can ye tell me, fisher laddies,*
What's gotten into the heads o' the haddies?"

—o—

(4) "*Stove him weel wi' wine an' spice,*
And butter in the bree;
I'se warrant he'll ken neist time
A feather frae a flee."

TABLE III.

(5) "*Fair fa' your honest, sonsie face,*
     Great chieftain o' the puddin' race."
—o—

(6) "*John Anderson, my jo,*
     Cum in as ze gae by,
     An' ze sall get a sheip's head
     Weel baken in a pie."
—o—

(7) "*An' first they ate the white puddin's,*
     An' syne they ate the black."
—o—

(8) "*Gie me lock brose, brose,*
     Gie me lock brose and butter."
—o—

(9) "*They a', in ane united body,*
     Declared it a fine fat howtowdie."
—o—

(10) "*He pang'd himsel' fu' o' collops an' kail,* (11)
    (12) *Syne whang'd at the bannocks o' barley-meal.*"
—o—

(13) "*It was fed wi' fouth o' gerse an' oats,*
     An' was wirried an' sauted at Johnnie Groat's."
—o—

(14) "*My heart's in the Highlands, my heart is not here,*
     My heart's in the Highlands, a-chasing the deer."

———

TABLE IV.

"*There's bread an' cheese at my door-check*
An' pancakes the riggin' o't."

"ORDER OF THE TOASTS AT THE GATHERIN' ON
THE 138 OWERCOME OF 22D JULY 1706.

" 1. The Majestie o' this Realm, being the Land o'
Cakes.

2. The Memorie o' the Last Queen o' Scotland.

3. The Cassin o' the Wanchancie Covenant.

4. The Abolition o' a' Assessments an' Blackmails.

5. A speedie Parliament in the Parliament House.

6. The Abolishment o' Stake Nets, an' the Restoration o' the auld Manier o' Fishin'.

7. A Dour Douncome to the Gadgers, an' a Kittle
Cast to the Customs.

8. The Buirdly Barons o' the Borders, an' the Auld
Road to Carlisle.

9. The Laird o' Raasay and Commissioners o'
Benachie.

10. True Thomas o' Ercildoune, Sir David Lyndsay
o' the Mount, an' a' the Famous Scottish Menstrils."

" *Nota bene.*—The farder order o' the ceremonie at the
pleasour o' the companie."

With the toasts, on the occasion of the "denner,"
were intermingled many of the Chairman's most
delightful songs—some of them being composed
for the occasion—together with other songs, hardly
less delightful, by a favourite Scottish landscape-
painter,* now, alas! no more; and with the irresist-

---

* D. O. Hill, R.S.A.

ible stories of another Scottish artist,* who, happily,
still survives to charm his countrymen alike with
his word- and colour- painting. It is needless to
say that the night was one of unequalled mirth
and enjoyment, and that the "pleasour o' the companie" protracted the "order o' the ceremonie"
till a late, or rather an early, hour.

Outram was often urged to publish, but he
always evaded the request. In the year 1851,
however, he was induced to print, for private
circulation, his Legal Lyrics, under the title,
'Legal Lyrics and Metrical Illustrations of the
Scotch Forms of Process; one hundred copies
printed for Private Circulation.' The edition was
limited, accordingly; and the excellence and originality of the contents were so greatly appreciated
by the more immediate friends to whom copies
were presented, that they were besieged on all
hands by requests for perusal; and at many social
meetings it was considered one of the chief attrac-
tions of the evening to hear some of the Lyrics
read or sung. None enjoyed them more than the
then acknowledged heads of the literary and intel-
lectual society of Edinburgh. One literary friend †
so much delighted in "The Process of Augmen-

---

* Sir Daniel Macnee, also now (1887) dead.
† The late Dr William Chambers of Edinburgh.

tation," that he used to have parties at his own house, where it was sung by the guests, in the characters and costumes of the Minister, the various Heritors, and the Lords of Session. The Minister's tune, composed by the author, is printed in this volume. Lord Rutherfurd was particularly enchanted with "The Process of Wakenin," as possessing a wonderful combination of pathos and drollery. Professor Wilson, Lord Cockburn, and many other admirers, likewise had their special favourites in the lyrical volume.

These Legal Lyrics, as yet so imperfectly circulated, have been much talked of, and the whole of them are included in the present volume. It is to be regretted that Outram never carried out his intention of writing some others, as indicated by certain fragments found among his manuscripts. One of these, intended to illustrate the Law of Lien, has the following graphic commencement :—

If ye've been up ayont Dundee,
Ye maun hae heard about the plea
That's raised by Sandy Grant's trustee
   For the mill that belang'd to Sandy.
For Sandy lent the man his mill,
An' the mill that was lent was Sandy's mill,
An' the man got the len' o' Sandy's mill,
   An' the mill it belang'd to Sandy.

> A' sense o' sin an' shame is gone,
> They're claiming noo a lien on
>   The mill that belang'd to Sandy.
> But Sandy lent the man his mill,
> An' the mill that was lent was Sandy's mill,
> An' the man got the len' o' Sandy's mill,
>   An' the mill it belang'd to Sandy.

The gossip of the Parliament House as to a flirtation (said to have commenced on the wrong side) between parties not usually brought together, gave rise to some verses entitled "The Macer's Daughter," of which the two following only have been preserved :—

> " 'Twas not his form, 'twas not his face,
>   'Twas not his eloquence, that caught her ;
> It was his name in every case
>   That gained the heart of the macer's daughter.
>
> 'Twas not her eye, or ruby lip,
>   Or teeth, like pearls in purest water ;
> He'd ne'er have touched her finger's tip
>   Had she not been the macer's daughter."

When his friend, the late Thomas Mackenzie, advocate, afterwards Lord Mackenzie, was rapidly rising as a junior at the bar, he received the honorary appointment of Counsel for the Woods and Forests, which gave rise to a song being commenced, called

THE WOODS AND THE FORESTS.

Are they accents of love, or the words of command ?
'Tis the voice of a lady—the first in the land—
Saying, " Trusty Mackenzie, I'll give you a fee,
If you'll roam through the woods and the forests with
   me.

" And, Tom, may it not be hereafter your pride,
As snugly you sit by your happy fireside,
To tell little Tommy, who sits on your knee,
How you roamed through the woods and the forests
   with me ?

And when you shall part with your bombasine gown.
And in ermine and silk on the Bench shall sit down,
Won't the great Lord Mackenzie remember with glee
How he roamed through the woods and the forests
   with me ?"

Other *disjecta membra* of a similar description
might be quoted, and some additional poems might
perhaps, with care, be selected from the MSS.;
but the task is delicate where the author himself
did not contemplate publication ; and, in the meantime at least, what is here given must suffice.

H. G. B.

ADDENDUM.

By LORD DEAS.*

THE relatives of the author have to lament the unexpected death of the accomplished editor of this little volume just when it was on the eve of being given to the public. It was to him a labour of love to select from the more ample manuscript volume, in which many of the author's compositions had luckily been preserved, those of which the humour and spirit were most likely to be apprehended and appreciated by readers who were not familiar with the characters and incidents which called them forth. The devotedness of the editor to his all but overpowering judicial duties—discharged with herculean strength and herculean success—necessarily superseded, to a great extent (although it never altogether prevented), the indulgence of his literary tastes and habits, and retarded the selection which, for a long period, he had at heart, of the specimens now given of the genius of his early and attached

---

* Mr Outram's brother-in-law.

friend, whom he enthusiastically admired, and whose uneventful life and genial character he has briefly recorded in the foregoing Introductory Notice.

As may be gathered from that notice, it was not unusual with the author to surprise his friends, at the social board, by effusions in which some of themselves (while ample justice was done to their solid qualities and acquirements) were, at same time, made the objects of an under-current of irresistible humour, which compelled them to join in a smile or a laugh at their own expense, and thereby covered the modest confusion which the admiring regard insinuated or expressed to-wards themselves, in their presence, might other-wise have occasioned.

In one of these effusions, of which the editor himself was the subject, his somewhat remarkable size and physical prowess were made the foil to carry off an expression of personal attachment, as well as appreciation of his powerful intellect, which was then—now some thirty years ago—well known to all who had adequate means of judging. Among the pieces proposed to be published, the editor, from motives of delicacy, had not included this one; but the relatives of the author, in now re-

cording their gratitude to the editor, trust that
they may be pardoned by his surviving friends
for the liberty they take in here presenting it to
the indulgent reader.

THE TZAR KOLOKOL.

(TUNE—" *The Misseltoe Bough.*")

In Russia there is, as all travellers tell,
Near the Kremlin, at Moscow, a ponderous Bell,
Called " King of the Bells" its fame to extol,
Or, in Muscovite language, the Tzar Kolokol.

'Tis made of all metals—gold, silver, and tin—
For each wealthy Russian some jewel cast in;
And the poor never rested till something they stole
To assist in compounding the Tzar Kolokol.

The furnace was fed by the young and the old;
The maid gave her ear-rings, the miser his gold;
For all knew 'twould be for the good of the soul
To give what they could to the Tzar Kolokol.

Full nine months passed over before it was cast,
But out came the mountain of metal at last,
And tribes from the tropics, and tribes from the pole,
Came as pilgrims to look at the Tzar Kolokol.

With ropes and with pulleys they hoisted the mass,
And they made it a tongue of some ten tons of brass,

And the world waited trembling to hear the first toll
From the King of the Bells,—from the Tzar Kolokol.

But that toll never came, for the rafters gave way,
And the ponderous giant was rolled in the clay;
And the fatal result was a wide gaping hole
That was broke in the side of the Tzar Kolokol.

We've a Bell in this country,—the King of Bells too;
Of metal as various, and temper more true,—
A sort of a giant—though, upon the whole,
He's not quite so big as the Tzar Kolokol.

It took nine months to cast him; and as for his tongue,
'Tis as brazen as theirs is, though much better hung;
And I'm sure we all feel 'tis good for the soul
To do what we can for our Tzar Kolokol.

Though he's never been hung yet, and never may be,
His voice has been heard o'er the earth and the sea,
And long may such music continue to roll
From the King of our Bells, from the Tzar Kolokol.

May the King live for ever, a Persian request
Which we make in behalf of our much-honoured
    guest;
May we oft pledge a bumper, and oft drain a bowl,
To the health of our Bell, to our Tzar Kolokol.

NOTE ON LETTER OF INVITATION, AND BILL OF FARE.

THE reference in the letter of invitation to "that wanchancie Covenant" (the Treaty of Union between England and Scotland), represents the intense feelings of objection and opposition to the Union which extensively prevailed in Scotland before the Treaty was made in 1707, and which continued to exist among many of the Scotch people till after the Rebellion of 1745. Much curious information on the subject will be found in Defoe's History of the Union, and of the proceedings and negotiations which preceded it. Sir Walter Scott alludes to these feelings in ' Rob Roy,' where, it may be remembered, Andrew Fairservice vehemently denounces the Union, while the shrewd and pawky Bailie shows a full appreciation of the benefits to flow from it to both countries.

The dishes which form the bill of fare are humorously indicated in the snatches of songs and sayings of the *menu*. They are generally old Scotch dishes, some of which are now scarcely known.

(1) This is "hotch-potch," which continues to be a favourite Scotch dish. The Shepherd in the 'Noctes Ambrosianæ' calls it "an emblem of the haill animal and vegetable creation."

"*Intil't*" is "in it."

The story goes that a Southron, who had greatly relished the soup, wished to learn from the cook how it was prepared, and she replied as in the text, "There's peas intil't," &c. He could make nothing of "intil't," which he perhaps thought was one of the articles used, and re-peatedly asked, "But *what's intil't?*" All, how-ever, he could extract from the somewhat angry cook was, "I have tell't ye already; there's peas intil't," &c.

(2) Leek-soup, commonly called "cock-a-leekie," is indicated. This is another prime Scotch soup, and according to Sir Walter Scott in the 'Fortunes of Nigel,' it was deemed fit for the royal table in the days of "King Jamie," who, after the marriage of "Glenvarlochides and pretty Peg-a-Ramsay," says—"*Surge, carnifex*—Rise up, Sir Richard Moniplies of Castle-Collop! And, my lords and

lieges, let us all to our dinner, *for the cock-a-leekie is cooling.*"

(3) This is a dish designated (*Scottice*) " crappit heads." It is composed of minced beef, with a considerable proportion of suet and some oatmeal, flavoured with chopped onions or leeks, and any other sweet herbs, and salt and pepper. The mess, when well mixed of the usual consistency of sausage, is stuffed into the heads or skulls of large haddocks, and is roasted in a Dutch-oven till sufficiently cooked. When properly made and seasoned it is a savoury dish.

(4) The reference in the lines, to knowing "neist time a feather frae a flee" (fly), and, in the Letter of Invitation, to "the trouts o' Lochleven," indicate a stew of Lochleven trout, caught by the fly in angling.

(5) A Scotch haggis is here referred to. It is prepared of similar materials to those used for "crappit heads," which are stuffed into the stomach of the sheep (called the "haggis-bag"), and the aperture being firmly sewed, it is boiled till sufficiently cooked. As the haggis-bag, if well filled, swells from the boiling of its contents, and the steam produced, it is often much swollen when brought to table, and should be opened carefully by a small incision, otherwise

its contents may squirt out, to the damage of
the table-cloth, and perhaps of the carver.

A description is given in the 'Noctes Ambrosianæ'—(Professor Wilson's Works, 1855,
vol. ii. p. 134)—of the danger of opening the
"haggis-bag" rashly. Christopher North, Tickler,
and the Shepherd have sat down to dinner, and
the Shepherd says :—

" ' I'll carve the haggis.'

" *North.* ' I beseech you, James, for the love of
all that is dear to you, here and hereafter, to hold
your hand. Stop! stop! stop!'

" *('The* SHEPHERD *sticks the haggis, and the
table is speedily overflowed."* A ludi-
crously comic scene is then pictured
of the sufferings of the party from
the flooding of the room, and of their
narrow escape from being drowned
in haggis.)*

(6) This is a sheep's-head pie. It is usually
prepared from the head of a fat tup, the wool of
which has been singed or burnt off to give it a
special flavour, which perhaps none but a Scotch-
man esteems.

(7) White puddings are prepared much in the
same way as ' crappit heads," the materials being

equal parts of oatmeal and suet. Black puddings have some blood added to the materials.

(8) Brose is made by pouring boiling water on toasted oatmeal, and stirred, as the water is poured in, by a blunt knife or the end of a spoon, till it is of the consistency of porridge or pudding. If the water has previously been used for boiling a round or rump of salt beef and greens, the dish is called "kail-brose"—lauded in the old song—

> "O the kail-brose of old Scotland !
> O for the Scottish kail-brose !"

(9) A "howtowdie" is a well-grown barn-door chicken.

(10) "Scotch collops" consist of slices of beef with the fat, stewed in a stewing or frying pan, with onions and pepper and salt.

(11) "Kail" is a soup of good stock, thickened with minced greens, and a little flour, till it is of sufficient consistency.

(12) Barley-meal "bannocks" are rolls or cakes of barley-meal toasted on a girdle.

(13) A salted Orkney goose is the dish indicated. It is usually cooked by boiling.

(14) A haunch or other dish of red-deer venison is referred to.

LEGAL AND OTHER LYRICS

THE ANNUITY.

AIR—"*Duncan Davidson.*"

I GAED to spend a week in Fife—
 An unco week it proved to me—
For there I met a waesome wife
 Lamentin' her viduity.
Her grief brak out sae fierce and fell,
I thought her heart wad burst its shell,
And—I was sae left to mysel'—
 I sell't her an annuity.

The bargain lookit fair eneugh—
    She just was turned o' saxty-three;
I couldna guessed she'd prove sae teugh,
    By human ingenuity.
But years hae come, and years hae gane,
And there she's yet as stieve's a stane—
        The limmer's growin'
          young again,
        Since she got her
          annuity.

        She's crined awa' to
          bane an' skin,
        But that it seems
          is nought to
          me;
        She's like to live—al-
          though she's in
        The last stage o'
          tenuity.
        She munches wi'
          her wizened
          gums,
        An' stumps about
          on legs o'
          thrums,

But comes — as sure as
    Christmas comes—
  To ca' for her annuity.

She jokes her joke, an'
    cracks her crack,
  As spunkie as a growin'
    flea—
An' there she sits upon my
    back,
  A livin' perpetuity.
She hurkles by her ingle-side,
An' toasts an' tans her
    wrunkled hide—
Gude kens how lang she yet
    may bide
  To ca' for her annuity!

I read the tables drawn wi' care
    For an Insurance Company;
Her chance o' life was stated there,
    Wi' perfect perspicuity.
But tables here or tables there,
She's lived ten years ayont her share,
An's like to live a dizzen mair,
    To ca' for her annuity.

I gat the loon that drew the deed—
    We spelled it o'er right carefully :—
In vain he yerked his souple head,
    To find an ambiguity :

        It's dated—tested—
          a' complete—
        The proper stamp—
          nae words delete—
And diligence, as on decreet,
    May pass for her annuity.

Last Yule she had a fearfu' hoast—
    I thought a kink might set me free :
I led her out, 'mang snaw and frost,
    Wi' constant assiduity.
But Deil ma' care—the blast gaed by,
And missed the auld anatomy ;
It just cost me a tooth, forbye
    Discharging her annuity.

I thought that grief might gar her quit—
    Her only son was lost at sea—
But aff her wits behuved to flit,
    An' leave her in fatuity !
She threeps, an' threeps, he's livin' yet,
For a' the tellin' she can get;
But catch the doited runt forget
      To ca' for her annuity !

If there's a sough o' cholera
    Or typhus—wha sae gleg as she?
She buys up baths, an' drugs, an' a',
    In siccan superfluity !
She disna need—she's fever proof—
The pest gaed o'er her very roof;
She tauld me sae—an' then her loof
      Held out for her annuity.

Ae day she fell—her arm she brak,
    A compound fracture as could be ;
Nae Leech the cure wad undertak,
    Whate'er was the gratuity.

It's cured!—She handles't like a flail—
It does as weel in bits as hale;
But I'm a broken man mysel'
    Wi' her and her annuity.

Her broozled flesh, and broken banes,
    Are weel as flesh an' banes can be.
She beats the taeds that live in stanes,
    An' fatten in vacuity!
They die when they're exposed to air—
They canna thole the atmosphere;
But her!—expose her onywhere—
    She lives for her annuity.

If mortal means could nick her thread,
    Sma' crime it wad appear to me;
Ca't murder—or ca't homicide—
    I'd justify't,—an' do it tae.
But how to fell a withered wife
That's carved out o' the tree o' life—
The timmer limmer daurs the knife
    To settle her annuity.

I'd try a shot.—But whar's the mark?—
    Her vital parts are hid frae me;
Her backbane wanders through her sark
    In an unkenn'd corkscrewity.

She's palsified—an' shakes her head
Sae fast about, ye scarce can see't;
It's past the power o' steel or lead
    To settle her annuity.

She might be drowned;—but go she'll not
    Within a mile o' loch or sea;—
Or hanged—if cord could grip a throat
    O' siccan exiguity.
It's fitter far to hang the rope—
It draws out like a telescope;
'Twad tak a dreadfu' length o' drop
    To settle her annuity.

Could pushion do't?—It has been tried;
    But, be't in hash or fricassee,
That's just the dish she can't abide,
    Whatever kind o' *goût* it hae.
It's needless to assail her doubts,—
She gangs by instinct—like the brutes—
An' only eats an' drinks what suits
    Hersel' an' her annuity.

The Bible says the age o' man
    Threescore an' ten perchance may be;
She's ninety-four;—let them wha can
    Explain the incongruity.

She should hae lived afore the Flood—
She's come o' Patriarchal
   blood—
She's some auld Pagan, mum-
   mified
   Alive for her annuity.

She's been embalmed inside and out—
   She's sauted to the last degree—
There's pickle in her very snout
   Sae caper-like an' cruetty;
Lot's wife was fresh compared to her:
They've kyanised the useless knir—
She canna decompose—nae mair
   Than her accursed annuity.

The water-drap wears out the rock
    As this eternal jaud wears me:
I could withstand the single shock,
    But no the continuity.
It's pay me here—an' pay me there—
    An' pay me, pay me, evermair:
I'll gang demented wi' despair—
    I'm *charged* for her annuity!

Wishes

(OF A MISANTHROPE).

AIR—"*O doubt me not*" (*Moore's Melodies*).

I WISH I was a *Woman!*
Wi' nought to do but dance an' dress,
    An' think mysel' sae bloomin',
An' kaim my hair afore the glass;
    To greet when my feet
Werena just sae sma' as I wad like,
    An' ne'er feel a care
Though the cobbler should nae discount strike :—

I'd spend my days in wearin' claes,
 An' my gudeman should pay the bill:
An' if he raised an unco fraise,
 I'd greet an' say I wasna weel!

I wish I was a *Hero!*
To spend my life in fire an' din,
 An' murder like King Nero,
An' never think it was a sin:
 I'd soon tak a toon,
An' wi' the spoil I wad mak free,
 An' style it in a bulletin
A great an' glorious victory!
 I'd write how brave my men behaved,
 An' how the field was won by me:
An' to my king and country leave
 To say what my reward should be.

I wish I was a *Lawyer!*
To ken what conscience ought to be,
 An' no remember a' year
My friends reduced to poverty;
 To be glad instead o' sad
When mithers weep, an' sons look pale,
 An' say grace o'er a case,
As honest men do o'er their kail.

"Go to the court o' last resort
For the sake o' your poor family."
" The Lords sustain ! " My client's gane—
He's ruined—but I've got my fee !

I wish I was a *Brute Beast !*
To live in some sequestered vale,
Frae friends and loves remote placed,
An' ne'er see man, an' wag my tail !
To chow on a knowe
A' the herbs, an' flowers, an' grassy blades,
An' tread ower the head
O' gowans never touched wi' spades :
I'd never see a friendly face,
Sae nae friend wad prove fause to me ;
I'd never ken the human race,
Nor ever curse humanity !

I wish I was a *Bottle !*
O' brandy, rum, or what you please,
In some frequented hôtel,
Where gude souls tak their bread an' cheese ;
To fill out a gill
For some puir chield that wants a trade—
Or pass o'er the hass
O' some blythe rantin', roarin' blade ;

An' while unscrewed, I'd sit an' brood,
　　An' think mysel' weel blessed to ken
That when I dee'd I'd spend my bluid
　　To purchase joy for honest men!

THE FACULTY ROLL.

In regard to this and the other lyrics which may be classed as "Legal," it may be interesting to non-professional readers to know something of the gentlemen of the Scottish Bar who are referred to, and to have explanations of the technical terms which occur. These are given in the notes appended.

The Faculty of Advocates is a very ancient body, not formally incorporated, but having most of the qualities and privileges of a corporation. Its members have the right of pleading causes in the Court of Session and High Court of Justiciary, and the other Scottish Courts, and they have, generally, the same position and duties as Barristers have in the Supreme Courts of England. The Faculty is presided over by a Dean and a Vice-Dean, the offices of both being honorary. Its members form an important branch of the Scottish "College of

Justice," which was instituted in May 1532, in the reign of King James V. The Judges of the Court of Session, which was established in the same year, are members of the College, having the title of "Senators"; and the members of the incorporation of Writers to the Signet, and of the Solicitors before the Supreme Courts, who act as Agents in the conduct of causes, are also members.

The Faculty has a noble library. It contains about 300,000 volumes, comprehending books in every department, and is enriched by many rare ancient MSS., and fine specimens of early printing on vellum—many of both exquisitely illuminated in colours as brilliant as when they left the hands of the artist.

The Faculty also administer a charitable institution.

The late Mr George Chalmers, a citizen of Edinburgh, who died in 1836, bequeathed the residue of his estate, amounting to a large sum, to "the Honourable the Dean and Faculty of Advocates," for the purpose of founding and maintaining a "hospital for sick and hurt." The fund was invested by the Faculty, and allowed to accumulate for some years, and by prudent investments it was largely augmented. Ultimately the house and grounds of Lauriston, adjacent to the Western Meadows, were purchased, and a handsome and commodious hospital, containing free wards for male and female patients, and a few wards in which, in addition to free medical attendance, home comforts may be afforded to patients able and willing to pay a very moderate board, was erected, and opened in 1864.

The beneficence of Mr Chalmers is appropriately commemorated by the names of " Chalmers Hospital " and " Chalmers Street," given to the hospital and dwelling-houses erected on part of the ground.

" The Faculty Roll," which follows, contains the names of a considerable number of the Advocates who were in practice in the years between 1830 and 1834, when Mr Outram was himself a member, and about which date the poem appears to have been written. The Faculty then consisted of nearly 400 members, of whom a comparatively small number are mentioned in the Roll. Very few of those mentioned now survive, and of course the " Roll " does not include any of the eminent men who have since been ornaments of the Bar, and ultimately of the Scottish Bench.

THE FACULTY ROLL

AIR—"*Ye Mariners of England.*"

YE Barristers of England,
　Your triumphs idle are,
Till ye can match the names that ring
　Round Caledonia's Bar.
Your *John Doe*, and your *Richard Roe*,
　Are but a paltry pair:
Look at those who compose
　The flocks round Brodie's Stair; [1]
Who ruminate on Shaw and Tait, [2]
　And flock round Brodie's Stair.

Although our *Brough'm* you've stolen,[3]
    To brush your Chancery—
He may be spared—our hoary *Baird* [4]
    Can sweep as clean as he;
And though you've got some kindly *Scotts*,
    To breathe your southland air,
We've the rest, and the best,[5]
    To stand by Brodie's Stair—
To garrison old Morison,[6]
    To stand by Brodie's Stair.

We'll still stand by our colours—
    Our *Brown, Reid, White,* and *Gray ;* [7]
We'll still extol our Northern Lights—
    You've seen their distant *Rae.*[8]
We still can boast of glorious names,
    Who love their country's fare,
And ne'er roam from their *Home,*[9]
    But study Brodie's Stair—
The pages con of Morison,
    And study Brodie's Stair.

Should enemies e'er venture
    To threaten us with war,
We'll rouse broad Scotland to our aid,
    From *Dingwall* to *Dunbar.*

The *Lothians, Ross,* and *Sutherland* [10]
   The powers of hell would dare
To the field, ere they'd yield
   One step of Brodie's Stair—
One foot of Erskine's Institute,[11]
   One step of Brodie's Stair.

The insolent invaders
   Should never move *Shank More ;* [12]
Our *Marshall's Steele,* the knaves should feel,[13]
   Within their bosom's core.
Have at them with a plump of *Spiers,*[14]
   And if that shock they bear,
Let the thieves meet our *Neaves,*[15]
   Ere they tread on Brodie's Stair—
Ere their foot pollute the Institute
   Of Erskine or of Stair.

We've some things worth defending,
   And that our foes shall see ;
Though ours is not a land of gold,
   'Tis the land of *Ivory* [16]—
And hearts behind our *Greenshields* beat,
   Than Ophir's stores more rare—

Ready still, come who will,
　　To fight for Brodie's Stair—
Resolved each Section to defend,
　　Of Erskine or of Stair.

Our *Hall* is all surrounded
　　By *Forrest*, *Loch*, and *Shaw* [17]—
A *Park*, such as you never trod,
　　A *Hill* you never saw.[18]
We rest among the summer *Hay*,
　　Beside the *Gowan* fair,[19]
With a *Rose* at our nose,
　　While we think on Brodie's Stair,
Or ponder on old Morrison,
　　Or think of Brodie's Stair.

We gather *Wood* and *Burnett*,[20]
　　When bleak December blows;
We're snug within, although without
　　The *Wilde* is *White* with snows.[21]
Our *Taylor*, and our *Hozier*,[22]
　　Defy the wintry air—
And the while to beguile,
　　We run through Brodie's Stair—
With Thomson's Acts, through Lord Kames' Tracts,
　　And Fountainhall, and Stair.[23]

We've three *Milnes*, and six *Millers*,[24]
   Although no meal we make ;
We've two *Weirs*, and a *Lister* large,[25]
   Although no fish we take ;
A *Horsman* too, without a horse [26]—
   A *Hunter*, but no hare—
Yet our *Horn* wakes the morn,
   With a note from Brodie's Stair,
While echoes court the full report
   Of Morrison or Stair.

Our table's poorly furnished—
   Our *Cook* has little toil—
Sometimes a fowl to *Currie*,
   Sometimes a joint to *Boyle* ;[27]
But still *Cheape's* head and *Trotters* is [28]
   The dish beyond compare—
To suggest Shaw's Digest,
   And the sweets of Brodie's Stair—
To give a zest to Shaw's Digest,
   And the sweets of Brodie's Stair.

For wisdom, where's the mortal
   Who claims to be our peer,
When Solomon was David's son.
   And *Davidson* is here ?

But for religion !—*Clerks*, alas ![29]
   And *Bells* we have to spare[30]—
But of faith, not a breath
   Is heard near Brodie's Stair;
Our most devout have Dirleton's Doubts,[31]
   As well as Brodie's Stair.

When politicians wrangle,
   We shun the idle brawl;
We've but one *Torrie* in our ranks,[32]
   And ne'er a Whig at all.
The schoolmaster abroad may roam—
   For him we do not care,
Because we've the *Tawse*,[33]
   And the rules of Brodie's Stair—
The lessons sage of Erskine's page,
   And the rules of Brodie's Stair.

And still as merry Christmas
   Concludes our peaceful year,
Our *Pyper* lends his minstrelsy.
   Our bounding hearts to cheer.
Poor as we are, for his reward,
   A *Penney* we can spare,
Though we've got but one *Groat*,[34]
   And some notes in Brodie's Stair—

Some doubtful bills in Dallas' Styles,
    And some notes in Brodie's Stair.

Our live-stock's scarce ; we have but
    A solitary *Hog ;*[35]
One *L'Amy* on his *Trotters* stumps,[36]
    Secure from *Wolf* or dog.[37]
But still whene'er he wanders forth
    We dread a *Tod* is there,
On the watch for a catch
    Should he slip from Brodie's Stair,
Or seek his food in Spottiswood,
    Or slip from Brodie's Stair.

But, Barristers of England,
    Come to us lovingly,
And any Scot who greets you not
    We'll send to Coventry.
Put past your brief, embark for Leith,
    And when you're landed there
Any wight with delight
    Will point out Brodie's Stair ;
Or lead you all through Fountainhall,
    Till you enter Brodie's Stair.

THE MULTIPLEPOINDING.

THE " process " or suit which bears this name is one peculiar to the law of Scotland. It may be resorted to in various circumstances, the most usual one being the case of several different parties claiming, on various grounds, the same fund. The claimants may stand in different positions. One may hold an assignment of the fund, which may or may not have been validly completed. Others may have made attachments of the fund, by a process which is known in Scotch law as "arrestment," by which money or movable or personal property is attached. Difficult questions frequently arise as to which of the claimants may have the preferable or best right to the fund, and for the solution of these a multiplepoinding is the appropriate suit.

In the case of a deceased party, who may have disposed of his estate by a deed of settlement in favour of trustees, questions frequently arise as to the interpretation, or the effect, of the provisions of the deed, and in such cases his trustees may institute a multiplepoinding for the purpose of having the construction or the effect of the deed settled, and the estate divided, under judicial sanction. In this suit, all parties claiming interest in the fund or estate, are cited into Court to maintain their respective claims. The person by whom the suit is instituted is technically called " the raiser," and the parties cited are termed " the claimants." The person to whom the fund belongs is also cited as a party for his interest, to see that the fund is properly disposed of. He is technically called the " common debtor." The judgment of the Court determines which parties have the best right, and ordains the fund to be paid to them; and, on payment of the fund or estate, which is technically called the " fund *in medio*," in accordance with the judgment of the Court, the " raiser " is judicially discharged or exonerated.

A great variety of questions may arise for discussion under the competing claims of " the claimants," and a multiplepoinding may thus include many different forms or kinds of suits, such as an action or suit of " declarator," un-

der which a person seeks to have any special
right judicially declared or established; or a suit
of "reduction," under which a person seeks to
have a deed or obligation set aside; or a suit of
"suspension," under which a party seeks to have
execution suspended or superseded. Hence a multiplepoinding is said in the song to—

"Combine *every comfort* that litigants know."

When the suit comes on for discussion before
the Judge, the name by which it is known—usually
the name of the pursuer or plaintiff, and of the
defendants or one of them—and the names of the
different counsel engaged in it, are called out by
the "macer" or mace-bearer in attendance at the
bar of the Judge. In former days the names were
called by the macer in a loud voice, and some old
practitioners may yet remember one red-faced and
pot-bellied little macer, who used to call the names
in a loud singing tone, which resounded through
the whole large Hall—a usual combination being,

"Maist-er *Fran*-cis Jeff-rey —
Maist-er *Hen*-ry Co-bran."

If the claimants are numerous, a number of
counsel may be engaged, and in the song a considerable number are so represented.

The Multiplepoinding.

AIR—"*O the Roast-Beef of Old England!*"

HURRAH for the Multiplepoinding! hurrah!
What land but our own such a gem ever saw?
Tis Process of Processes—Pride of the law—
  Hurrah for the Multiplepoinding!
  The Multiplepoinding, hurrah!

To the rich, to the poor, to the high, to the low,
'Tis open to all who a title can show

It combines every comfort that litigants know—
    Hurrah for the Multiplepoinding !
    The Multiplepoinding, hurrah !

No matter in what shape your claim may emerge,
By Petition or Summons, Suspension or Charge,
Reduction, Declarator, all may converge
    And conjoin in the Multiplepoinding—
    The Multiplepoinding, hurrah !

From the north, from the south, from the east, from
    the west,
Come claimants, each deeming his own claim the
    best,—
What myriads of lawyers are then in request
    To manage the Multiplepoinding !
    The Multiplepoinding, hurrah !

Hark ! hark ! what the deuce is that Macer about ?
What means his prolonged, diabolical shout ?
Does the man mean to call the whole Faculty out ?
    Hurrah ! 'tis the Multiplepoinding—
    The Multiplepoinding, hurrah !

See ! see ! how the lawyers all start at the sound !
See ! see ! how the agents from place to place bound !

See! see! how their clerks flash like lightning
  around!
      Hurrah! 'tis the Multiplepoinding—
      The Multiplepoinding, hurrah!

They rush to the Bar like the waves of the sea—
They swarm like a hive on the branch of a tree—
They'll smother the Judge—he is not a Queen
  Bee—
      Hurrah for the Multiplepoinding!
      The Multiplepoinding, hurrah!

But the storm is composed, and there's silence at
  last—
The lawyers look grave, and the Judge looks
  aghast,
And the short-hand Reporter prepares to write fast
      His notes of the Multiplepoinding—
      The Multiplepoinding, hurrah!

There the Dean stands profound as the depths of the
  sea;[1]
And Snaigow—as smooth as its surface could be;[2]
And Rutherfurd—sharp as the rocks on the lee;[3]
      All fee'd for the Multiplepoinding-
      The Multiplepoinding, hurrah!

And there stands M'Neill, "with his nostril all
 wide,"[4]
And Ivory's eyes glisten fierce by his side ;
And Cunninghame's there with his papers untied,[5]
  And dreams of the Multiplepoinding—
  The Multiplepoinding, hurrah !

And More and Buchanan have come at the call,
And Marshall, and Pyper, and Whigham and
 all—
And Peter the Great looks to Adam the Tall[6]
  To open the Multiplepoinding—
  The Multiplepoinding, hurrah !

'Twas Janet M'Grugar, ship-chandler, Dundee,
Became moribund in the year twenty-three,
And disponed her estates all to Nathan M'Ghee,
  Who claims in the Multiplepoinding—
  The Multiplepoinding, hurrah !

That she had not disponed in *liege poustie* was
 plain,
For she ne'er went to kirk or to market again—
So maintains her apparent heir, Donald M'Bean,[7]
  Who claims in the Multiplepoinding—
  The Multiplepoinding, hurrah !

Now Donald M'Bean was in debt to the knee,
And so, it appeared, too, was Nathan M'Ghee,
And Janet herself had by no means been free,
    And so cam' the Multiplepoinding—
    The Multiplepoinding, hurrah !

And what with arrestments, where'er funds could be,
And charges on bill and extracted decree,[8]
And hornings and captions—you'll easily see
    'Twas a beautiful Multiplepoinding—
    The Multiplepoinding, hurrah !

But where are the claimants, and how have they
    sped ?
See you shrivelled matron, as hueless as lead,—
'Tis a liferent she claims—and she's on her death-
    bed !
    Hurrah for the Multiplepoinding !
    The Multiplepoinding, hurrah !

Her deep indignation she cannot repress,
Though her tongue is scarce able her griefs to ex-
    press—
She swears 'tis an action of " double distress."[9]
    Hurrah for the Multiplepoinding !
    The Multiplepoinding, hurrah !

The landlord claimed rent—and he'll best tell you
　　how
He got into the process by poinding a cow ;
His hypothec is quite hypothetical now [10]—
　　　Hurrah for the Multiplepoinding !
　　　The Multiplepoinding, hurrah !

The Suspender was bothered to such a degree [11]
That he went and suspended himself from a
　　tree ;
The Arrester's in jail—no forthcoming can he
　　　Obtain through the Multiplepoinding—
　　　The Multiplepoinding, hurrah !

One brought a Reduction—but he has retired, [12]
Reduced to extremes his worst foe ne'er desired.
The Adjudger—as well as the Legal's expired. [13]
　　　Hurrah for the Multiplepoinding !
　　　The Multiplepoinding, hurrah !

No more will the poor Heir-Apparent appear—
By way of a seisin they've seized all his gear ;
He's absconded—and now his Retour, it is clear,
　　　Can't be hoped through the Multiplepoind-
　　　　ing [14]—
　　　The Multiplepoinding, hurrah !

" *In medio tutissimus!* "—this might be true
When Phœbus instructed, and Phaëton flew;
But the fund, though *in medio*, has gone to pot
    too [15]—
        Hurrah for the Multiplepoinding!
        The Multiplepoinding, hurrah!

The Creditor's credit is utterly gone—
And he, whom they call Common Debtor, alone
Has uncommon good luck—he's got off with his
    own! [16]
        Hurrah for the Multiplepoinding!
        The Multiplepoinding, hurrah!

SOUMIN AN' ROUMIN.

THE extract from 'Stair's Decisions' prefixed
to the song, does not do much to elucidate its un-
couth and unintelligible title, and was doubtless
intended, not to elucidate, but to add to the per-
plexity.

The action or suit, which is unknown in modern
times, was one which might be instituted by any
proprietor of lands adjacent to a commonty in
which he and other proprietors had a common
or joint right, for the purpose of ascertaining and
fixing what extent of pasturage or other right
each proprietor was entitled to exercise in the
commonty. The old lady in question had been
advised to resort to it, in order to ascertain how
many sheep or cattle she was entitled to put
upon the commonty for pasturage. "Soums" and
"roums" are old Scotch terms in land rights, and
give the suit its peculiar name.

"Where divers heritors have a common pasturage in one commonty, no part whereof is ever ploughed, the said common pasturage may be *soumed* and *roumed*, that all the *soums* the whole commonty can hold may be determined and proportioned to each *roum* having the common pasturage, according to the holding of that *roum*."
—*Case of the Laird of Drumelzier, Stair's Decisions,* II. 678.

AIR   *"Hooly and Fairly."*

My Grannie!—she was a worthy auld woman ;
She keepit three geese an' a cow on a common.

Puir body!—she sune made her fu' purse a toom
     ane,
By raising a Process o' Soumin an' Roumin,
        Soumin an' Roumin—
        By raising a Process o' Soumin an' Roumin.

A young writer lad put it into her head;
He gied himsel' out for a dab at the trade—
For guidin' a plea, or a proof, quite uncommon
And a terrible fellow at Soumin an' Roumin,
           Soumin an' Roumin, &c.

He took her three geese to get it begun,
And he needit her cow to carry it on,
Syne she gied him her band for the cost that was
     comin',
And on went the Process o' Soumin an' Roumin,
           Soumin an' Roumin, &c.

My Grannie she grieved, and my Grannie she
     graned,
As she paid awa' ilk honest groat she had hained;
She sat in her elbow-chair, glow'rin' and gloomin'—
Speakin' o' naething but Soumin an' Roumin,
           Soumin an' Roumin, &c.

She caredna for meat, and she caredna for drink—
By night or by day she could ne'er sleep a wink;
"O Lord, pity me, for a wicked auld woman!
It's a sair dispensation this Soumin an' Roumin."
　　　　　　　Soumin an' Roumin, &c.

In vain did the writer lad promise success—
Speak of Interim Decrees, and final redress;
In vain did he tell her that judgment was comin'—
"It's a judgment already this Soumin an' Roumin!"
　　　　　　　Soumin an' Roumin, &c.

The Doctor was sent for—but what could he say;
He allowed the complaint to be out o' his way;
The Priest spak' o' Job—said to suffer was
　　human—
But she said "Job kent naething o' Soumin an'
　　Roumin."
　　　　　　　Soumin an' Roumin, &c.

The Priest tried to read, and the Priest tried to
　　pray,
But she wadna attend to ae word that he'd say;
She made a bad end for sae guid an auld woman—
Her death-rattle sounded like "Soumin an' Roumin,"
　　　　　　　Soumin an' Roumin, &c.

E

I'm Executor—heir-male—o' line—an' provision,—
An' the writer lad says that he'll manage the seisin;*
But of a' the Estate, there's naething forthcomin',
But a guid-gangin' Process o' Soumin an' Roumin,

Soumin an' Roumin, &c.

---

* The seisin, as already explained, was a writ to complete
the heir's title to the property which had proved so dis-
astrous to his poor old grandmother.

The Old True Blue.

AN HISTORICAL BALLAD.*

AIR—"*Captain Glen.*"

OME, Buff and Blue chaps,
    here's my claw,
    You're good souls in your way;
But ere you compare your Man
    of Law
To old Admiral Milne, belay
    your jaw,
    And hear what I've to say,
            Brave boys!
    And hear what I've to say.

---

* Written on the occasion of a parliamentary election contest for the Leith burghs, between the late Admiral Milne and the then Lord Advocate, John Archibald Murray, and sung through the streets by a disabled sailor.

'Tis forty years and more this day
  (Short time it seems to me !)
Off Guadaloupe our frigate lay,
The Frenchman skulked in Mahout Bay,
  Beneath the battery,
                        Brave boys !
  Beneath the battery.

We cruised about from place to place,
  And swept the ocean free ;
At last, ashamed of the disgrace,
Mounseer put on his fighting face,
  And ventured out to sea,
                        Brave boys !
  And ventured out to sea.

He trusted to his metal's weight,
  And to his crowded crew ;
We cheered him as he hove in sight,
For though our numbers were not great,
  Our men were all true blue,
                        Brave boys !
  Our men were all true blue.

We fought him on that glorious day,
    While we could man a gun ;
Each mast and spar was shot away,
But though a shattered hulk we lay,
    Our colours ne'er went down,
                        Brave boys
Our colours ne'er went down.

We fought him on that glorious day,
    Till our decks were drenched in gore ;
But hot and hotter grew the fray,
Till at length the Frenchman's heart gave way,
    And he doused the tricolor,
                        Brave boys !
And he doused the tricolor.

We lay like logs upon the tide,
    Not a boat or oar had we ;
I stood by our youthful leader's side—
    "Come, follow me, my lads !" he cried,
    And plunged into the sea,
                        Brave boys !
And plunged into the sea.

He swam aboard of the noble wreck,
　We followed with a will :
I stood at his side on the Frenchman's deck—
I stood by him then, and, come what like,
　I'll stand by Admiral Milne,
　　　　　　　　Brave boys !
　I'll stand by Admiral Milne.

I've seen his glory grow since then,
　With his increasing years ;
His faithful shipmate still I've been,
Till a splinter cost me my larboard fin
　At the taking of Algiers,
　　　　　　　　Brave boys !
　At the taking of Algiers.

I'll stand by him now as then I stood,
　And I'll trust him now, because
It's like he'll labour to do us good,
Who never scrupled to spill his blood
　In aid of his country's cause,
　　　　　　　　Brave boys !
　In aid of his country's cause.

As for that bumboat lawyer craft
  That you have got in tow,
A seaman would rather trust to a raft
Than a hulk that looms so large abaft,
  If a gale should come to blow,
           Brave boys!
 •If a gale should come to blow.

Belike with speeches fair he'll try
  To *gammon** me and you:
Come! off, ye swab! if you wish to shy;
But here stands one that would rather die
  Than shrink from the Old True Blue,
           My boys!
  Than shrink from the Old True Blue,

---

* A *canard* had been got up that his lordship had joined in
a game at backgammon in the steamer, between London and
Leith, on a stormy Sunday.

Y Tweedside a-standin',
Wi' lang rods our hands in,
In great hopes o' landin' a Saumon were we;
I took up my station,
Wi' much exultation,
While Morton* fell a-fishin' farther doun upon the
lea.

---

* Charles Morton, W.S., a school and lifelong friend of
Outram's.

Across the stream flowin'
My line I fell a-throwin',
Wi' a sou'-wester blowin' right into my ee ;
I jumpt when my hook on
I felt something pookin' ;
But upon farther lookin' it proved to be a tree.

But deep, deep the stream in,
I saw his sides a-gleamin',
The king o' the Saumon, sae pleasantly lay he ;
I thought he was sleepin',
But on further peepin',
I saw by his teeth he was lauchin' at me.

The flask frae my pocket
I poured·into the socket,
For I was provokit unto the last degree ;
And to my way o' thinkin',
There's naething for't but drinkin',
When a Saumon lies winkin' and lauchin' at me.

There's a bend in the Tweed, ere
It mingles with the Leader—

If you go you will see there a wide o'erspreadin'
    tree ;
        That's a part o' the river
        That I'll revisit never—
'Twas there that scaly buffer lay lauchin' at me.

THE PROCESS OF AUGMENTATION.

— ---

Soon after the Reformation, the Judges of the
Court of Session were appointed commissioners,
with jurisdiction as a Court, in questions of teinds
or tithes. A certain portion of the teinds had by
the Scottish Parliament been set apart in each
parish as the stipend of the clergyman holding the charge — the remainder of the teinds
remaining in possession of the different heritors
or proprietors of the lands from which teind
is legally exigible, or of the Crown, or a donee
of the Crown called "the Titular," as in right
of the estates of the Romish Church. When
a clergyman considers his stipend too small, he
may institute a suit in the Court of Teinds for
having it increased; and the amount of stipend
which may be fixed in that suit, remains as
the stipend for a period of twenty years; after

which, if circumstances warrant it, a further increase may be sought from the Court of Teinds.

The stipend is paid by the heritors or proprietors of lands in the proportions fixed by the Court in what is termed a "scheme of locality." The suit is termed one of "augmentation, modification, and locality," and the heritors or proprietors in the parish and the Crown or Titular are cited as defendants in it, as they hold the teinds subject to payment of the stipend, and to any augmentations of it which the Teind Court may from time to time see cause to grant.

The Process of Augmentation.

The Minister States his Case to a Tune of his own Composing for which see p. 92.

WHOEVER shall oppose my claim for augmentation,
    I'll hold amongst my foes —
    Whoever shall oppose :

I'll deem him one of those who seek their own dam-
   nation,
Whoever shall oppose my claim for augmentation.

Though some may hold their lands *cum decimis*
   inclusis,[1]
      Secure from my demands—
      Though some may hold their lands;
Enough's in other's hands, who have no such excuses—
Though some may hold their lands *cum decimis*
   inclusis.

'Tis fully twenty years since my stipend was augmented,—
      A time of want and fears!
      'Tis fully twenty years;
In silence and in tears my griefs I have lamented;
'Tis fully twenty years since my stipend was augmented.

'Tis partly paid in Bear, and partly paid in Barley;[2]
      Though few such crops now rear,
      'Tis partly paid in Bear;

Though Wheat and Oats elsewhere are now grown
    regularly,
'Tis partly paid in Bear, and partly paid in Barley.

My glebe is small and poor, and my parish is pro-
    digious.
        How long shall I endure !
        My glebe is small and poor.
No error, I am sure, was ever more egregious.
My glebe is small and poor, and my parish is pro-
    digious.

I have no means but those. A small mortifica-
    tion
        Just keeps my wife in clothes.[3]
        I have no means but those.
If I might be jocose, I'd say on this occasion
I have no means but those—a *great* mortification.

Then whoever shall oppose my claim for augmenta-
    tion,
        I'll hold amongst my foes—
        Whoever shall oppose ;

I'll deem him one of those who seek their own dam-
nation,
Whoever shall oppose my claim for augmentation.

The Heritors Defend themselves to the Tune of "Judy Callaghan."

FIRST HERITOR.

And hang me if I don't
Oppose your augmentation !
My Lords, you surely won't
Condemn me to starvation.
I couldn't give a rap
To purchase immortality,
More than that fat old chap
Draws under the last locality.

Chorus of Heritors—Uh ! uh ! uh !
Nae wonder we're in sic a rage—
He wants the hale o' the teind,
Parsonage and Vicarage.[4]

SECOND HERITOR.

She'd readily pay her merk
    Upon ony just occasion;
But she lives ten miles frae the kirk—
    An' she's of another persuasion.
He ought to scrutineese
    The errors that have perverted her—
An' she'll pay him whatever ye please
    As soon as he has converted her.

      Chorus—Uh! uh! uh! &c.

THIRD HERITOR.

My father mortified
    A field of about ten acre—
But he scarce had signed the deed
    When his spirit was aff to his Maker.
Had the minister shown less greed,
    I didna mean to object to it—
But now I hope to see't
    Reduced *ex capite lecti* yet.

      Chorus—Uh! uh! uh! &c.

FOURTH HERITOR.

He says, that frae the teinds
    He is but puirly pensioned;
But he's ither ways an' means,
    Though he'd rather they werena mentioned.
He kens the ways o' a'
    The wives in his vicinity,
An' weel can whillywha
    A rich, auld, sour virginity.

Chorus—Uh! uh! uh! &c.

FIFTH HERITOR.

He'll croon to ane on death,
    Until her een are bleerit—
An' lecture anither on faith,
    Till she's like to gang deleerit.
An' thus he mak's a spoil
    O' fatuous facility,
An' works into the Will
    O' dottrified senility.

Chorus—Uh! uh! uh! &c.

SIXTH HERITOR.

Every time (an' that's ance a-year)
    That his wife's in the hands o' the howdie,
He sets the hale parish asteer
    For things to favour her crowdie.
An' this ane sends jelly an' wine,
    An' that ane sends puddin's an' pastries,
Till she—like a muckle swine—
    Just wallows in walth an' wasteries.

     Chorus—Uh! uh! uh! &c.

SEVENTH HERITOR.

He warns us to beware,—
    For if we're caught in transgression,
It's his duty to notice't in prayer,
    Or bring us afore the Session;
But a turkey, or a guse,
    Or some sic temporalities,
Can mak' a braw excuse
    For a' our wee carnalities.

     Chorus—Uh! uh! uh! &c.

EIGHTH HERITOR.

The time he fixes for
    Parochial visitation,
Is aye our dinner-hour—
    An' he's sure to improve the occasion.
An' siccan a stamack he has !
    You'd think he'd ne'er get to the grund o' it ;
An' he tells us that flesh is grass—
    Just after he's swallowed a pund o' it.

Chorus—Uh ! uh ! uh ! &c.

ALL THE HERITORS TOGETHER.

Then, oh, my Lords, don't grant
    The smallest augmentation !
His pleading's nought but cant,
    Perversion and evasion.
Don't give a single rap
    ('Twere worse than prodigality)
More than that fat old chap
    Draws under the last locality.

Chorus—Uh ! uh ! uh ! &c.

THE LORDS MODIFY.

JUDICIAL MADRIGAL.—Air—"*Now is the Month of Maying.*"

The Court on this occasion
Of solemn consultation,
    Fol lol de rol, &c.—
With deep sense of their high
Responsibility,
      Thus modify:[5]
        Fol de rol, &c.

We'll first allow him yearly
Ten pecks of Meal,—as clearly
      Equivalent
        To the full extent
Of stipend paid in Bear;

Though, lest he that deny,
We'll add, for certainty,
A boll of Rye.
Fol de rol, &c.

One chalder, in addition,
Of Oats, would seem sufficient;
And an increment
To that extent
We therefore modify,
With Barley as before.
Lord C.—" Oh ! half a chalder more."
Ho ! ho ! hi !—(*Judicial laughter.*)

The process now must tarry
Till the Junior Ordinary
Proceed to prepare,
With his usual care,
A scheme of locality.[6]
And, having done its turn,
The Court will now adjourn
Instantly.
Fol de rol, &c.

(*The Lords adjourn.*)

THE HERITORS REJOICE.

Hurrah for the Court o' Teinds!
    Hurrah for the Tithe Commission!
We couldna done better if friends
    Had taen up the case on submission.
His teeth he now may gnash
    O'er his matters alimentary;
The Lords have settled his hash
    For anither fifth part of a century!
        Ha! ha! ha!
      They've done for his venality!
        Hurrah! hurrah! hurrah!
      For the rectified locality!

Had he an offer fair,
    Or rational propounded,
For twa three chalders mair
    We'd gladly hae compounded.—
A boll o' Meal a-year
    We'd readily hae sent it him—
Forbye his pickle Bear,
    If that could hae contented him.
        Ha! ha! ha!
      The clod o' cauld legality!
        Hurrah! hurrah! hurrah!
      For the rectified locality!

But he wad tak' nae course,
    Except to raise an action,
In order to enforce
    The most extreme exaction.
He's now got his decree—
    An' muckle he's the better o't!
But we'll tak' care that he
    Shall keep within the letter o't.
        Ha! ha! ha!
        The mass o' fat formality!
            Hurrah! hurrah! hurrah!
        For the rectified locality.

For not a single Ait,
    Nor yet a spike o' Barley,
Nor nip o' Meal, he's get
    Again irregularly.
His wife, neist time, may grane
    As friendless as the Pelican;
While he may dine his lane
    Forenent her empty jelly-can.
        Ha! ha! ha!
        The lump o' sensuality!
            Hurrah! hurrah! hurrah!
        For the rectified locality!

                    (*Exeunt Heritors.*)

THE MINISTER CONSOLES HIMSELF.

Though I have been beset by roaring Bulls of
    Bashan,
      There is some comfort yet,
      Though I have been beset.
'Tis well that I'm to get a little augmentation,
Though I have been beset by roaring Bulls of
    Bashan.

I've many other cares that press on my attention.
      My Manse requires repairs [7]—
      I've many other cares,—
Nay! common-sense declares it needeth an exten-
    sion.
I've many other cares that press on my attention.

The rooms are far too small, and fewer than be-
    seemeth.
      Should sickness e'er befall,
      The rooms are far too small;
We can't have beds for all when next my helpmeet
    teemeth.
The rooms are far too small, and fewer than be-
    seemeth.

A wing on either side, of decent elevation—
　　　　Proportionably wide—
　　　　A wing on either side—
Would suitably provide for our accommodation,—
A wing on either side, of decent elevation.

My byre requires new walls—my milk-house a new
　　gable.
　　　　To stand the wintry squalls,
　　　　My byre requires new walls.
New mangers and new stalls are needed for my
　　stable.
My byre requires new walls—my milk-house a new
　　gable.

If all this be not done unto my satisfaction,
　　　　Before a year has run,—
　　　　If all this be not done,—
All compromise I'll shun, and raise another action—
If all this be not done unto my satisfaction.

　　　And whoever did oppose, &c.—(*Exit muttering.*)

DISTANT CHORUS OF HERITORS.

Ha ! —ha ! —ha !

Curs ——mean ——scality !

—rah ! —rah ! —rah !

Rec ——fied ——cality !

THE MINISTER'S TUNE.

The Law of Marriage.

THOUGHTS AT SEA.

O MARRIAGE!—tell me if you truly are
    A Deity, as poets represent ye!
Or are you, as the Institutes declare,
    Nothing but a *consensus de presenti?*
No matter!—I espoused a maid of twenty
By promise, and a process *subsequente.*[1]

We married without contract; but our rights
    Were all defined within the year and day.
A youngster came, one o' the cold spring nights—
    I hardly had expected him till May.
My wife did well—in fact as well as could be;
The baby squeaked, and all was as it should be.

The darling's eyes were dark and deeply set—
  My wife's and mine were light and round and
    full;
His hair was thick and coarse and black as jet,
  While ours was thin and fair and soft as wool;
I knew 'twas vain to play the rude remonstrant,
For *Pater est quem nuptiæ demonstrant.*

The am'rous youth may fervidly maintain
  That marriage is a cure for every trouble;
The feudalist may learnedly explain
  When its avail is single and when double:[2]
Its sole avail to me, I grieve to say it,
Was debt—without the wherewithal to pay it.

And debt brings duns. My dun was of a sort
  That never can desist from persecution.
He brought my case before the Sheriff Court—
  My debt, they told him, needed constitution.
'Twas false ! He knew—I knew it to my curse—
It had the constitution of a horse.

But the decree went out, and I went in—
  And in the jail lived *more debitorum;*
Yet though I lost my flesh I saved my skin,
  By suing for a Cessio Bonorum.

I got out, naked as an unfurred rabbit.
The Lords dispensed, they told me, with the habit.[3]

I went to seek my wife, but she had fled,
    And had not left a single paraphernal;
But matrimonial law, upon my head
    Seemed destined still to pour its curse eternal.
I had indeed obtained a separation
From bed and board—no prospect but starvation !

But bed and board are things worth striving for,
    So I bethought me of the pea and thimble :
But people had grown wiser than of yore,
    And all in vain I plied my fingers nimble.
I then attempted Vitious Intromission,[4]
And was immediately conveyed to prison.

And here again I lay upon my oars ;
    A Hermit keeps his cell—my cell kept me.
No letters came to me of Open Doors ;
    Criminal letters, though, came postage free,
The air I breathed just added to my cares,
Reminding me of coming Justice Ayres.[5]

And come they did!   And therefore am I now
    Upon thy wave, old Ocean—Sydney bound!
And here the partner of my youthful vow,
    Among the fourteen yearers have I found;
Here are we (though not just as when we courted)
Again united and again transported.

The Reform Bill.

AIR—

"*Merrily danced the Quaker.*"

H ! weary fa' Reform an'
　　Whigs !
That ever they were
　　invented !
An' wae's me for my auld gudeman,
　　He's fairly gane demented :
He grunts and growls frae morn to night
　　About pensions an' taxation :
He's ruined wi' meetin's got up for the gude
　　O' the workin' population.

The fient a turn o' wark he'll do
　　To save us frae starvation ;
He leaves his Horse to sort the Coo,
　　For he maun sort the nation.

The fient he'll do but read the news—
  An' he reads wi' sic attention,
That his breeks are a' worn out in a place
  Which I'm ashamed to mention.

He gangs to publics ilka night,
  An' ilka groat he'll spend it,
An' how he gets hame in siccan a plight
  I canna comprehend it.
An' then my sons, like three wee Hams,
  Laugh at their drucken daddie,
As down on the floor wi' a clout he slams,
  Wi' een like a Monday's haddie.*

Afore the Whigs began their rigs,
  He was anither creature;
His een were bright as stars at night,
  An' plump was every feature.
His brow was like the lily white,
  His cheeks as red as roses;
He had a back like Wallace wight,
  An' a thicker beard than Moses.

---

* The Monday's haddock must have been caught at least on
the Saturday, and hence the condition of its eyes.

But now he's lost his comely look,
    An' lost his stalwart figure;
His een are sinkin' into his head,
    An' his nose is growin' bigger.
His houghs are gane, he's a' owertane,
    And fusionless as a wether;
His back sticks out, an' his wame fa's in—
    An' he's a' reformed thegither!

Oh! dinna ye mind, my auld gudeman,
    When first we cam' thegither,
How cheerily our wark gaed on,
    How pleased we were wi' ither?
Our lives passed away like a Sabbath-day
    When the distant bells are ringin';
An' your breath was sweet as the new-mawn hay,
    An' no like a rotten ingan.

Oh! just to think what ye were then,
    An' now what ye are brocht to!
Ye're far waur aff than ever you were
    Before Reform was thocht o':
For then, when you wanted a sark to your wame,
    Ye made an unco wark, man;
But what's to be done wi' you now, when you
    hae nae
    A wame to pit in your sark, man?

Oh ! gin ye wad but mind your pleugh,
　　An' mind your empty pockets,
'Twere wiser-like than drink an' read
　　Your een out o' their sockets.
Leave them that ken to mak' the laws—
　　An' while your breeks will mend, man,
Just leave the nation to look to itsel',
　　An' look you to your hinner end, man !

John and Jean.

Antenuptial.

JOHN SINGS OF JEAN.

AIR—"*Bonnie wee thing.*"

ONNIE Jeanie!
  Artless Jeanie!
  Rosy, cosy Jeanie!
    Wert thou mine!
  How wad I adore you!
  What could I do for you!
  Think on what I swore
      you—
    See if I repine!

Try to vex me,
Pester or perplex me—
A' your little sex may,
  To bother ane o' mine!

Wreck me—break me—
Lick me—kick me—
Only let me think, the
Wee bit foot was thine.

—

JEAN SINGS OF JOHN.

(*In lines varied from old Scottish Ballads.*)

When bonnie young Johnnie went over the sea,
He said there was naething he liket like me.
He sang an' he whistled while haddin' the pleugh,
Though of gowd an' of gear he hadna eneugh.

But noo he has gotten a hat an' a feather—
An' its hey! brave Johnnie, lad! cock up your beaver.

His kin are for ane o' a higher degree,
What has he to do wi' the like o' me?
Although I am bonnie, I amna for Johnnie,
An' werena my heart licht I wad dee.

(*Dreams.*)

Lang hae we parted been,
Johnnie my dearie;

Noo we hae met again,
　Laddie, lie near me !
Near me !　(*Suddenly wakening.*)　Dear me !
　Did ony ane hear me ?
Could Johnnie been listenin' ?
　Dear me !—Oh dear me !

Postnuptial.

JOHN TELLS OF JEAN.

(*To a tune of his own composing.*)

Oh ! what a deevil, a deevil, a deevil !
　Oh ! what a deevil is Jean !
The life o' a deevil I lead wi' the deevil,
　An' she cares deevil a preen !

She dauds wi' the poker, but no at the coals,
Her tongue an' her temper are out o' a' rules ;
She dings at my head wi' a dizzen o' shools,
　And then she bawls out, " Mind your een !"
　　　　　　　Oh ! what a deevil, &c.

She seizes the kail-pat, an' I get my share ;
The stools spend the best o' their time in the air,
An' sittin' is no the right
    use for a chair,
  As I an' my shattered
    banes ken.

      Oh ! what a deevil, &c.

I never come right down my stair, stap by stap,
For she aye flings me head over heels frae the tap ;
An' when I gang down wi' a horrible slap,
  She bids me come soon back at e'en !
      Oh ! what a deevil, &c.

She plays at the ba' wi' my head every day,
An' when I fa' ower she cries out—Hurrah !

An' she's got a great cuddie-heel to her shae,
 An' I've got a patch for my een!
     Oh ! what a deevil, &c.

It's a miracle she's murdered nane o' the weans,
For she plays rowley-powley wi' them at my shins,
An' she says that it's punishment for's a' at ance,
 Like killin' twa dogs wi' ae bane.
     Oh ! what a deevil, &c.

I'm sae muckle accustomed to lounders and licks,
That when I'm asleep she canna wake me wi'
 kicks,
Though her fit is as heavy as baith o' Auld
 Nick's,
 No countin' the weight o' her shoon.
    . Oh ! what a deevil, &c.

She dauds at me sae, whatever I do,
I'm just ae muckle lump through an' through,
An' every bit o' my body is blue,
 Except twa three bits that are green !
     Oh ! what a deevil, &c.

JEAN REFLECTS ON JOHN.

(*To the same tune.*)

Oh! what a deevil, a deevil, a deevil,
   Oh! what a deevil is John!
Dinna think me unceevil to ca' him a deevil,
   Till you hear how the deevil gangs on.

He snuffs, an' he smokes, an' he drinks, an' he
   chews,
Till he's donnard, an' daised, an' ayont ony use;
An' how he whiles finds his way hame to his house,
   Is to me just a phènomenon!
                    Oh! what a deevil, &c.

He fa's on the stair, an' he coups o'er the weans—
It's a miracle he's broken nane o' their banes,
As he bangs at the wa', or clytes doun on the
   stanes
   Wi' a weight that is twenty stane tron.
                    Oh! what a deevil. &c.

An' when wi' a fecht I hae got him to bed,
He lies crookit, an' pu's a' the claes to his side;

An' he's got evermair sic a cauld in his head,
That the neb o' him rins like a rone.
Oh ! what a deevil, &c.

When at last he's asleep, an' I'm just fa'in' o'er,
It wad be heaven's mercy if he'd only snore ;
But he first gives a squeak—then a grunt—then a
roar—
Like a bagpiper sortin' his drone.
Oh ! what a deevil, &c.

In the mornin', to rise to his wark he's sae
laith,
I whiles think he's sleepin' the slumber o' death ;
I've to kick and to paik till I'm clean out o'
breath,
Ere I get him to cry out " Ohone !"
Oh ! what a deevil, &c.

On pay-nights he'll come hame as white as a
clout,
Wi' his hat a' bashed in, an' his pouch inside
out ;
An' afore I can ask him what he's been about,
He fa's down as flat as a scone.
Oh ! what a deevil, &c.

Just last Sunday morning—O sic a disgrace !—
The very policeman that took him up, says,
That he never saw, in the coorse o' his days,
    Sic a shamefu' exposure as yon.

                    Oh ! what a deevil, &c.

The Banks o' the Dee.

AIR—"*Days o' lang syne.*"

I MET an auld man on the banks o' the Dee,
An' a merrier body I never did see;
Though Time had bedrizzled his haffits wi' snaw,
An' Fortune had stown his luckpenny awa',
Yet never a mortal mair happy could be
Than the man that I met on the banks o' the Dee.

O, ance he had plenty o' owsen an' kye,
A wide wavin' mailin an' siller forbye;
But cauld was his hearth ere his youdith was o'er,
An' he delved on the lands he had lairded before;
Yet though beggared his ha' an' deserted his lea,
Contented he roamed on the banks o' the Dee.

'Twas heartsome to see the auld body sae gay,
As he toddled adown by the gowany brae,
Sae canty, sae crouse, an sae pruif against care;
Yet it wasna through riches, it wasna through lear;
But I fand out the cause ere I left the sweet Dee—
The man was as drunk as a mortal could be!

AIR—"*Peggie is over ye Sie wi ye Souldier.*"—SKENE MS.

JENNY! puir Jenny! the flow'r o' the lea—
The blythesome, the winsome, the gentle an' free—
  The joy and the pride
  O' the haill kintra side—
She dee'd of a process o' Wakenin.*

---

  * When a suit in Court remains for a year, without procedure taking place, it is technically said to fall asleep. It may
be resuscitated by raising a summons or suit of "wakening."

Though her skin was sae smooth, an' her fingers sae
    sma',
She won through the hoopin'-cough, measles an'
    a'—
        She never took ill
        Frae fever or chill—
Yet she dee'd of a process o' Wakenin.

The case fell asleep when her Grandfather dee'd,
And few folk remembered it e'er had been plea'd.
        She never heard tell
        O' the matter hersel',
Till they sent her the summons o' Wakenin.

Jenny! puir Jenny!—though courted by a',
Only ane touched her heart—an' he bore it awa'.
        It had just been arranged
        That her state should be changed,
When they sent her the summons o' Wakenin.

She had plighted her troth—they had fixed on the
    day—
A' arrangements completed—nae chance o' delay ;
        She was thinkin' on this,
        And entranced wi' bliss,
When they sent her the summons o' Wakenin.

Her friends were sae kindly—her true-love sae
    prized,—
Surrounded by them, an' by him idolised;
        She had just passed the night
        In a dream o' delight,
When they sent her the summons o' Wakenin.

She fee'd the best counsel—what could she dae
    mair?
She read through the papers wi' sorrow an' care,
        But could only mak' out,
        That beyond ony doubt,
'Twas a wearifu' process o' Wakenin.

An' her friends that she thought wad be constant
    for aye,
Of course they grew scarce, an' kept out o' her way;
        For naebody ken'd
        How the matter wad end,
When they heard o' the process o' Wakenin.

An' her true-love for whom she wad gladly gien a',
Slid cauld frae her grasp like a handfu' o' snaw;—
        Sae she gied up the case,
        An' gied up the ghaist,
An' dee'd o' a process o' Wakenin.

"Ta reel o' Tullochgorum."

Cessio Bonorum.*

Air—" *Tullochgorum.*"

Come ben ta house, an' steek ta door,
An' bring her usquebaugh galore,
An' piper pla' wi' a' your pow'r
    Ta reel o' Tullochgorum.
For we'se be croose an' canty yet—
    Croose an' canty,
    Croose an' canty—
We'se be croose an' canty yet,
    Around a Hieland jorum.

* By the law of Scotland, a debtor imprisoned for debt, or
in certain equivalent circumstances, since imprisonment for
debt was abolished, may institute a suit of *cessio bonorum*.
Under it, the Court, if satisfied of the debtor's honesty and
inability to pay, may grant him protection against claims for
debts then existing, upon his making a conveyance of all his
means to a trustee for his creditors' behoof, and might grant
him liberation, if in prison.

We'se be croose an' canty yet,
For better luck she never met—
She's gotten out an' paid her debt
    Wi' a Cessio Ponorum!
        Huch! tirrum, tirrum, &c.

She meant ta pargain to dispute,
An' pay ta price, she wadna do't,
But on a Bill her mark she put,
    An' hoped to hear no more o'm.
Blythe an' merry was she then—
    Blythe an' merry,
    Blythe an' merry—
Blythe an' merry was she then
    She thought she had come ower 'm.
Blythe an' merry was she then—
But unco little did she ken
O' Shirra's laws, an' Shirra's men,
    Or Cessio Ponorum!
        Huch! tirrum, tirrum, &c.

Cot tamn!—but it was pad indeed!
They took her up wi' meikle speed—
To jail they bore her—feet an' head—
    An' flung her on ta floor o'm.

CESSIO BONORUM.

Wae an' weary has she been—
    Wae an' weary,
    Wae an' weary—
Wae an' weary has she been
    Amang ta Debitorum.
Wae an' weary has she been,
An' most uncivil people seen—
She's much peholden to her frien'
    Ta Cessio Ponorum!
        Huch! tirrum, tirrum, &c.

She took an oath she couldna hear—
'Twas something about goods an' gear,—
She thought it proper no to speer
    Afore ta Dominorum.
She kent an' caredna if 'twas true—
    Kent an' caredna,
    Kent an' caredna—
Kent an' caredna if 'twas true,
    But easily she swore 'm.
She kent an' caredna if 'twas true,
But scrap't her foot, an' made her poo,
Then, oich!—as to ta door she flew
    Wi' her Cessio Ponorum!
        Huch! tirrum, tirrum, &c.

She owed some bits o' odds an' ends
An' twa three debts to twa three friends—
She kent fu' weel her dividends
    Could paid anither score o'm.
Ta fees an' charges were but sma'—
    Fees an' charges,
    Fees an' charges—
Ta fees an' charges were but sma',
    Huch! tat for fifty more o'm!
Ta fees an' charges were but sma'—
But little kent she o' the law.
Tamn!—if she hasn't paid them a'
    Wi' her Cessio Ponorum!
        Huch! tirrum, tirrum, &c.

But just let that cursed loon come here
That took her Bill!—she winna swear,—
But, ooghh!—if she could catch him near
    Ta craigs o' Cairngorum!
If belt an' buckle can keep fast—
    Belt an' buckle,
    Belt an' buckle—
If belt an' buckle can keep fast,
    She'd mak' him a' Terrorem.

If belt an' buckle can keep fast,
Her caption would be like to last,
Py Cot!—but she would poot him past
    A Cessio Ponorum!
        Huch! tirrum, tirrum, &c.

Lady! Thine Eye is Bright.

LADY! thine eye is bright—
    Boast of it well,
While youth and delight
    In its fairy beam dwell:
Fast comes the hour
    When its light must away—
Potent the power
    That bids beauty decay.

Lady! thy lip is red—
    Be proud, lady, proud;
Rejoice ere its bloom is shed
    Under the shroud.
When the sod presses you,
    Pleasure is gone;
When the worm kisses you,
    Raptures are done.

Lady ! rejoice—
  Triumph has crowned you ;
List to the voice
  Of flatt'ry around you.
Forget that your bright day
  Brings darkness behind it ;
Forget while you may,
  You will soon be reminded !

What will I do gin my Doggie Dee?

AIR—"*O'er the hills an' far away.*"

On! what will I do gin my doggie dee?
He was sae kind an' true to me,
Sae handsome, an' sae fu' o' glee—
What will I do gin my doggie dee?
My guide upon the wintry hill,
My faithfu' friend through gude an' ill,

An' aye sae pleased an' proud o' me—
What will I do gin my doggie dee?

He lay sae canty i' my plaid,
His chafts upon my shouther-blade,
His hinder paw upon my knee,
Sae crouse an' cosh, my doggie an' me.
He wagged his tail wi' sic a swirl,
He cocked his lug wi' sic a curl,
An' aye snook't out his nose to me—
Oh ! what will I do gin my doggie dee?

He watched ilk movement o' my ee,
When I was glad he barkit tae;
When I was waefu', sae was he—
Oh ! I ne'er lo'ed him as he lo'ed me.
He guarded me baith light an' dark,
An' helpit me at a' my wark;
Whare'er I wandered there was he—
What will I do gin my doggie dee?

Nae ither tyke that you could meet,
Was ever fit to dicht his feet;
But now they'll hae a jubilee,
He's like to be removed frae me.

'Twas just yestreen my wife an' he—
Deil hae the loons that mauled them sae!
They're baith as ill as ill can be—
What will I do gin my doggie dee?

Elsie.

(*As sung by her boorish husband.*)

Air—"*Bobbin John.*"

Elsie's neat an' clean,
　Elsie's proud an' saucy,
Elsie's trig an' braw,
　Elsie is a lassie;
Elsie is a fule,
　Elsie's neives are massy,
Elsie's tongue is lang—
　Elsie is a lassie.

Elsie is my wife,
　Thinks to be the ruler:
Elsie is an ass,
　Thinks that I care for her;

Swears she'll keep the cash,
  Disna keep a boddle,
Wares it a' on dress,
  Ca's hersel' a model!

Elsie is a guse—
  I'll gang an' tell her,
I'll hae the house,
  I'll hae the siller ;
I'll haud my ain,
  I'll keep the causey ;
Elsie wear the breeks ?—
  Elsie is a lassie.

I've got a foot,
  Ken how to use it ;
If I gie a kick,
  She maun just excuse it.
I am a man,
  Strong built an' massy—
Elsie takes her chance,
  Elsie's but a lassie !

Dubbyside.

THE foam-flakes flash, the black rocks scowl,
The sea-bird screams, the wild winds howl;
A giant wave springs up on high—
"One pull for God's sake!" is the cry:
If struck, we perish in the tide—
If saved, we land at Dubbyside!

O Dubbyside! our peril's past,
And bliss and thee are reached at last!
As sprang Leander to his bride,
Half drowned, so we to Dubbyside!
What though we're drenched, we will be dried
Upon thy banks, sweet Dubbyside'

Are we in Heaven, or are we here,
Or in the Moon, or Jupiter?

These velvet Links, o' golfers rife,
Are they in Paradise, or Fife?
Am I alive, or am I dead,
Or am I *not* at Dubbyside?

Through Eden's groves there flowed a stream,
And there its very waters gleam—
Its pebbly bed, its banks the same,
Unchanged in all except the name,
Since Adam bathed in Leven tide,
While Eve reposed at Dubbyside!

And still it is a blissful spot,
Though Paradise is all forgot
The fairies shower their radiance here,
The rocks look bright, the dubs are clear;
Deem not that bush the forest's pride—
Remember, you're at Dubbyside!

Is that an angel shining there,
Or sea-nymph with her flowing hair,
Or Neptune's pearl-embowered bride
Kissing the foam-bells of the tide?
'Tis neither angel, nymph, nor bride—
'Tis Podley Jess of Dubbyside!

When this Old Wig was New.

AIR—" *When this old coat was new.*"

WHEN this old wig was new,
 The Barber raised his eyes
And blessed himself to view
 A wig so wondrous wise !
It was his pride—and, sooth,
 I proudly prized it too,
For I was but a youth
When this old wig was new.

But now my wig is old,
 And I am young no more ;
The course of time has rolled,
 And our career is o'er :

1

I'll mix no more with men
    As I was wont to do,
Nor see the days again
    When this old wig was new.

Oh, the days that I have seen,
    And the hours that I have passed,
And the pleasures that have been
    Too exquisite to last!
Before my eyes they pass
    In sweet though sad review—
I think of what I was
    When this old wig was new.

I think of times when far
    Aloof cold envy stood,
And brethren of the Bar
    Professed good brotherhood—
Not soulless etiquette,
    But friendship warm and true,—
With heart and hand we met
    When this old wig was new.

No greedy hand was then
    Projected for a fee ;
We held no servile pen
    To any lordly he :
And none of us demurred
    The poor man's cause to sue,
For honour was the word
    When this old wig was new.

Then truly was the age
    Of matchless eloquence,
And counsels deep and sage,
    And energy intense ;
And we had men of lore,
    And wit and fancy too,
For Wisdom's cup ran o'er
    When this old wig was new.

I've laughed until mine eye
    Has filled with tears of glee,
I've wept that fountain dry
    From very agony,
As the floods of Erskine broke,
    Or the sparks of humour flew
From the lips of those who spoke
    When this old wig was new.

But when our weekly toil
    Brought Saturday about,
Then all was one turmoil
    Of revelry and rout.

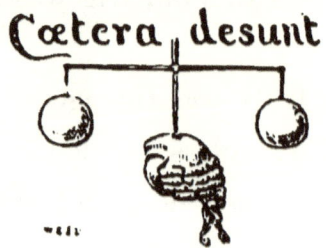

Cætera desunt

THE SIGN O' THE CRAW

(SENTIMENTS ATTRIBUTED TO A WELL-KNOWN FREQUENTER OF THAT INSTITUTION.)

AIR—"*Soldier's joy.*"

LET others sing the graces an'
    roose the jolly faces
O' a' the bonny lasses that
    ever were ava;
I'll rout wi' right gude will,
    about the joys I feel,
When sookin' at a gill at the
    Sign o' the Craw.
        Lal de dandle, &c.

I like meat unco weel, for my wame it can fill,
An' wantin' it I feel I could ne'er fend ava:
But why I wish to fend some folk hae never ken'd—
'Tis my staps that I may bend to the Sign o' the
    Craw.
        Lal de dandle, &c.

I'll acknowledge my belief, that to hae a tidy wife
Is a comfort to my life that I couldna forega;
For if she's worth a louse, she may surely keep the
    house
When I've gane to take a bouse at the Sign o' the
    Craw.

> Lal de daudle, &c.

I never a' my days liked to gang withouten claes,
An' a reason if you please I can readily shaw:
'Tis that when my siller's gane, my coat I then can
    pawn,
An' get anither can at the Sign o' the Craw.

> Lal de daudle, &c.

The last time I was sober, ae morning in October,
I foregathered wi' a robber wha clinked my cash awa :
But not e'en the hornèd deil frae me can ever steal
What I've gien them for a gill at the Sign o' the Craw.

> Lal de daudle, &c.

I wadna gie a sneeshin' to hear a blockhead screechin',
Himsel' an' ithers fashin', 'cause a lassie's ran awa';
Contented here I am, sae I'll e'en take aff my dram,
Till I fa' into a dwam at the Sign o' the Craw.

> Lal de daudle, &c.

My Wife has come ower to Cure Me.

Air—" *My Mither's aye glowerin' o'er me.*"

MY wife she's come ower to
cure me—
For naething on earth but
to cure me;
I was deein' o' ease, an' com-
fort, an' peace,
An' my wife has come ower
to cure me.
Nae doubt I was ill when
a' thing gaed weel,
An' I didna ken what was
gude for me;
My sleep was sae soun', an' my body sae roun';
But my wife has come ower—an' she'll cure me.

My wife has come ower to cure me,
My wife has come ower to cure me;
She cuist up her place where she gat meat an'
    claes,
An' she's come ower the water to cure me.
My cheeks were sae red, my heart was sae
    glad,
Bad symptoms they were to alarm me;
Preternatural fat, an' strength, an' a' that,
But my wife has come ower—an' she'll cure me.

My wife has come ower to cure me,
To show the affection she bore me;
I was decin' o' health, an' ruined wi' wealth,
When my wife came ower to cure me.
I rose wi' the lark, an' ate like a shark,
A' the joys o' the angels came ower me;
Outrageously right, stark mad wi' delight;
But my wife has come ower—an' she'll cure me.

My wife has come ower to cure me—
For no earthly cause but to cure me;
I was horridly weel—my banes hard as steel;
But my wife has come hame—an' she'll cure me.

Oh were she to die, what wad come o' me?
What spirits an' thrills wad devour me!
Ilka pap wi' the shool on the tap o' the mool,
Wad forbid her frae comin' to cure me.

Drinkin' Drams.

(BACCHANALIAN HEROICS.)

AIR— "*My Luve's in Germany.*"

[Since Mr Outram wrote the following verses, the temperance cause has made great progress, and deservedly so; but it is just possible that it will be the temperance people rather than the topers who will laugh most at this ironically humorous song.]

HE ance was holy,
An' melancholy,
Till he found the folly
    O' singin' psalms;
He's now as red's a rose,
An' there's pimples on his nose,
And in size it daily grows
    By drinkin' drams.

He ance was weak,
An' couldna eat a steak
Without gettin' sick
    An' takin' qualms;
But now he can eat
O' ony kind o' meat,
For he's got an appeteet
    By drinkin' drams.

He ance was thin,
Wi' a nose like a pen,
An' haunds like a hen,
    An' nae hams ;
But now he's round an' tight,
An' a deevil o' a wight,
For he's got himsel' put right
    By drinkin' drams.

He ance was saft as dirt,
An' as pale as ony shirt,
An' as useless as a cart
    Without the trams ;
But now he'd face the deil,
Or swallow Jonah's whale—
He's as gleg's a puddock's tail
    Wi' drinkin' drams.

Oh ! pale, pale was his hue,
An' cauld, cauld was his broo,
An' he grumbled like a ewe
    Without the rams ;
But now his broo is bricht,
An' his een are orbs o' licht,
An' his nose is just a sicht
    Wi' drinkin' drams.

He studied mathematics,
Logic, ethics, hydrostatics,
Till he needed diuretics
    To lowse his dams ;
But now, without a lee,
He could make anither sea,
For he's left philosophy
    An' taen to drams.

He found that learnin', fame,
Gas, philanthropy, an' steam,
Logic, loyalty, gude name,
    Were a' mere shams ;
That the source o' joy below,
An' the antidote to woe,
An' the only proper go,
    Was drinkin' drams.

Here I am.

Whaever's here that wishes a cure
   For mind, or wind, or limb,
Let him listen to mine—wi' me it's been sure—
   It'll be the same wi' him.
Whatever comfort failed me,
Whatever it was that ailed me,
Whatever was my plisky,
   Whatever dangers cam—
I tipp't aff a bottle o' whisky,
   An' here I am !

Ance I was ill, and to mak' up his bill,
   The Doctor cam like stour,
Wi' a forpit o' squills, an' laxative pills,
   My illness sair to cure.
He swore I was in a consumption—
I swore he had nae gumption ;

He said I might tak the riskie—
  I said I wad tak my dram, —
Sae I tipp't aff a bottle o' whisky,
  An' here I am !

When I was in love, my mettle to prove,
  My sweetheart behaved unco queer ;
She ance saw me fou, an' she ca'd me a sow,
  An' said I was portable beer !
Her love I cast aff a' houp o't,
Sae I ran to a linn to loup it—
But as I was rinnin' sae briskly,
  I thought I wad tak a dram—
Sae I tipp't aff a bottle o' whisky
  An' here I am !

I ance gaed aff, like a sober calf,
  To sail the warld round,
But as we cam' back, the ship was a wrack,
  An' we were just gaun to be drowned ;
The passengers lustily sang out,
The crew whomelled into the long boat,
An' how I got out o' the plisky,
  I dinna ken whether I swam—
But I tipp't aff a bottle o' whisky,
  An' here I am !

WE BE THREE
POOR BARRISTERS

ROUND—"*We be three poor Mariners.*"

WE be three poor Barristers,
    With minds but ill at ease,
Because we never are retained
    In any kind of pleas.
We pace the House around, around, around,
Where litigants abound, abound, abound,
        Where fees are rife,
        Yet for our life
We cannot take a pound, a pound, a pound.

Ah! little do their clients know,
    Who trust to legal skill,
What injury their doers do,
    Employing whom they will,
And leaving us around, around, around,

No chance to be renowned, renowned, renowned,
      Though we have store
      Of wit and lore
That might the world astound, astound, astound.

We wonder what their agents think—
      Or if they think at all—
Who still employ these little men,
      With voice so thin and small,
You scarce can hear a sound, a sound, a sound,
While we walk idly round, around, around—
            With lungs to make
            The rafters shake
And vaulted roofs rebound, rebound, rebound.

As for that clerk of evil fame,
      Accursèd let him be,
Who tempteth meaner souls than ours
      To plead for a half a fee—
With emphasis profound, profound, profound,
We execrate the hound, the hound, the hound,
            As to and fro
            Each day we go
Across the earthen Mound, a-Mound, a-Mound!

Yet not because we're thus forgot
    Down-hearted shall we be;
The pluckless soul may yield to grief—
    We'll live in jollity!
We'll pass the glass around, around, around,
And thus dull care confound, confound, confound,
        Nor heed the fee
        So long as we
With mirth and glee abound, abound, abound.

"Come, wed with a Lawyer!"

The Lawyer's Suit.

Air—"*For the lack of Gold.*"

Oh why, lady, why, when I come to your side,
Repulse your poor suitor with such haughty pride?
That you'll never wed with a Lawyer you swear—
But why so averse to a Lawyer, my dear?

Can it be, that because I have thought and have read,
Till my heart to the world and its pleasures is dead?
Pshaw! my heart may be hard, but then it is clear
Your triumph's the greater to melt it, my dear!

Can it be that because my eyes have grown dim,
And my colour is wan, and my body is slim?
Pshaw! the husk of the almond as rough may
    appear—
But what do you think of the kernel, my dear?

Would you wed with a Fop full of apish grimace,
Whose antics would call all the blood to your face?
Take me, from confusion you're sure to be clear,
For a Lawyer's ne'er troubled with blushes, my dear!

Would you wed with a Merchant, who'd curse and
    who'd ban
'Cause he's plagued by his conscience for cheating a
    man?
Take me, and be sure that my conscience is clear,
For a Lawyer's ne'er troubled with conscience, my
    dear!

Would you wed with a Soldier with brains made of
    fuel,
Who, defending his honour, is killed in a duel?
Take me, and such danger you've no need to fear,
For my honour is not worth defending, my dear!

Come, wed with a Lawyer! you needn't fear strife,
For since I have borne with the courts all my life,
That the devil can't ruffle my temper, I'll swear—
And I hardly think you could do't either, my dear!

My Nannie.

AIR—"*Carrickfergus.*"

My Nannie fell sick, an' my Nannie was deein',
My friends a' advised me for doctors to send ;
But she was sae grievin' me when she was livin',
That, troth, I had little desire she should mend.

I said I'd nae siller—they wadna come till her—
Sae I watched her wi' tenderest care by mysel' ;
But whate'er was the matter, the limmer got better,
And to my great sorrow she soon was quite well.

Wi' a jorum o' whisky I gat mysel' frisky,
An' said 'twas for joy to see her sae weel :
Says she—" How got ye that when you couldna buy
    med'cine ? "
An' gied me a thump wad hae murdered the deil !

Her passion near choked her—I ran for the doctor—
But she hardly had been a week under his care,
When he said—"Your wife's leavin' the land o' the
　　livin',—
I've done what I could, sir—I canna do mair."

"O Doctor!" says I, "Sir, you'd much better stay,
　　sir,
An' do what ye can for her—till she's quite gane!"
He plied her wi' physic, an' that made her sae sick,
That in less than a month Nannie graned her last
　　grane!

To the Doctor I handed twice what he demanded;
My friends a' advised me to marry again—
But quo' I, "I'll no marry again in a hurry,
For I canna forget my dear Nannie that's gane!"

The Holy Loch.*

Calm, calm, the blue lake silent lies,
   The sky without a breath to shake it;
The drowsy clouds nor fall nor rise—
   The earth's asleep, and none to wake it.
The sun glares with his fiery eye
   Upon the beauteous scene before him,
While green-robed Nature modestly
   Shrinks from such outrage of decorum.

The sun has gone, the day is done,
   The moon beams o'er the peaceful water,
High up above, looking such love
   As mother's o'er an only daughter.
In vain, in vain my ear I strain
   To catch the ripple of the billow.
I don't feel well—I'll ring the bell,
   And ask them just to shift my pillow.

* These were the last verses composed by the author.

Ensurance.

AIR —"*What can a Young Lassie.*"

The premium is ae thing—the duty's anither,
It comes a' thegither to saxty pound three,
An' ilk year at Yule it gars us sing dool—
It's a terrible pull on a poor family!
But the gudeman was failin' an' constantly ailin',
'Twas high time that his life insurèd should be;
And on ilk occasion it's some consolation
That we'll a' be provided for gin he should die.

IS THE HOUSE WARM YET?

It was an old Scotch custom—not yet wholly unknown—that a dinner or supper should be given by the head of the house, to a few choice and intimate friends, on the family entering a new place of residence. Such meetings were always highly convivial. The warmth or mirth of the party was held as a sort of forecast of the future character of the house, so the host did his best to promote the hilarity and enjoyment of his friends, while they showed their kindly sympathy in the warmth of their welcome to his new abode. Toasts of kind words and good wishes were drunk in flowing bumpers, and so the libations to Bacchus were not stinted. *Dulce est desipere in loco* was the joyous feeling. The new house was just the desired *locus*, and as the fun generally "grew fast and furious," something like the high-jinks of Pleydell and his jolly *confrères* in 'Guy Mannering' was usually the upshot. Such was a Scotch " house-heating " or " house-warming" fifty years ago.

The song seems to have been written, either to be sung at such a symposium given by Outram in a new residence, or, at a future convivial meeting in remembrance of it. The scenes described are of course fancy pictures, intended possibly to give some indication of each guest's turn of mind when abandoned to mirth and frolic.

Is the House Warm Yet?

AIR--"*When the house is rinnin' round about it's time enough to flit.*"

When there's joy in ilka heart, and there's mirth in
    every ee,
When we've burst the bands o' care and feel the
    spirit free,
An' we canna tell what house it is, we then may
    think it fit
To whisper to each other—Is the house warm yet?
      Is the house warm yet? is the house warm
        yet?
      It aye becomes the cozier the langer that we
        sit;
      An' till it's like an oven we will never steer
        a fit,
      Though we ask at ane anither—Is the house
        warm yet?

When Bell begins to falter in his boisterous career,[1]
And Mackenzie's merry voice begins to sound a little
    queer,[2]
And Hill's becoming tuneless[3]—we may the question
    pit,
In whispers to each other—Is the house warm yet?
        Chorus—Is the house warm yet? &c.

When Rhind begins, with husky throat, to overture
    the chair,[4]
And the joyous - hearted Crutherland seems quite
    o'ercome wi' care,[5]
And Ellis seems at sea[6]—we may then the question
    pit,
In whispers to each other—Is the house warm yet?
        Chorus—Is the house warm yet? &c.

When Macnee confuses Archie wi' the little Paisley
    boy,[7]
And Dunbar's tongue is motionless by sheer excess
    of joy,[8]
And Spens calls it doubly hazardous[9]—we then may
    think it fit
To inquire at ane anither—Is the house warm yet?
        Chorus—Is the house warm yet? &c.

When Salmond breaks his glass and seeks to justify
    the deed,[10]
And the Doctor frae Gartnavel tries to stand upon
    his head,[11]
And the landlord fa's asleep—we may then the ques-
    tion pit,
In whispers to each other—Is the house warm yet?
        Chorus—Is the house warm yet? &c.

And when the house is warmed at last, and frae it
    we have gane,
We maun haud a carefu' memory o' the road back
    again ;
An' o' friendship an' o' kindness we'll often tak a fit,
An' come rinnin' back to ask—Is the house warm
    yet ?
        Chorus—Is the house warm yet? &c.

An Appeal from the Sheriff.*

" Understood to allude to an appeal from the Sheriff's decision in a case
Mr Outram had with a gasfitter, who undertook to ventilate his
house, but made it nearly uninhabitable instead."

On this case Lord Cockburn wrote the following Epigram, the litigation
affording much merriment to all Mr Outram's legal friends :—

Not a room in the house the same climate can boast,
On the one side we freeze, on the other we roast ;
And if to the fireside your chair you should pull in,
Your back is in Lapland, your knees in Ben Coolin.†

SUSTAINS the pursuer's title !
Finds no irregularity in cital,
Therefore repels the defences,
    And in respect
    The stamp is correct,
Decerns for pursuer, with expenses.

---

* Notes on An Appeal from the Sheriff, see p. 223.
† A dreadfully hot place in Sumatra, East Indies.

Am I to be ruined by such drivel?
No! I'll see the pursuer at the devil;
'Tis only Henry Bell's decision—
    'Tis not too late
    To advocate,
And avoid this enormous lesion.

I'll go to the Court of Session,
And resist this most infamous oppression;
I'll retain both Monro and M'Kenzie,
    Fordyce, Handyside,
    And others true and tried,
And I'll put the pursuer in a frenzy.

But if Fortune in spite of them should fail me,
And neither law nor equity avail me,
I'll care not for either Division—
    Though I go to the court
    Of last resort,
I'll upset this preposterous decision.

On Hope.

Saw ye the snow-wreath,
  White on the hill?
Saw ye the wild lily
  Bloom by the rill?
Saw ye the star
  Light heaven only,
Gleaming afar,
  Lovely and lonely?

Hope's like the snow
  That falls from the sky:
Beauteous and holy,
  It dazzles the eye.
But with manhood comes sorrow,
  And hopes disappear;
And the snow-drop to-morrow
  Will melt to a tear.

Hope's like the lily
   That bloomed in the spring,
Wooing the breeze
   With its delicate wing.
Alas! the bright sun,
   In which it delighted,
Too powerfully burns,
   And the lily is blighted.

Hope's like the lone star
   In Eternity riding,
The trembling mariner
   O'er the deep guiding.
A dim earthly vapour
   Its glory hath crossed:
Hope has departed—
   The sailor is lost.

Forget not me.

Forget not me, my love,
  When others whisper thou art fair;
With honeyed words their lips may move,
  But love like mine is rare.

Forget not me, my love,
  When warmer eyes upon thee rest;
Their fire can ne'er so fervent prove
  As that within my breast.

Think not I doubt thy faith;
  The wreathy foam upon the sea,
Spread by the zephyr's gentlest breath
  Is not more pure than thee.

I well believe thee true,
   Thy heart will ne'er deceitful be :
But then that heart is tender too,
   For it was kind to me.

May not a tearful eye,
   A glowing cheek, and mournful air,
Break from thy friendly heart a sigh,
   And waken pity there ?

Ae Day I got Married.

AIR—"*They all take a sup in their turn.*"

AE day I got married—an' so you see
There of course was an end to peace wi' me;
Whenever I moved, Kate loosed her tongue,
An' when I replied, she took to the rung;
    So what between licking,
    An' scolding, an' kicking,
I hoped for rest but in the grave.

My wife was a woman—an' so you see
She was nae great shakes at constancy;
Sae a lawyer cam' and skreighed himsel' hoarse,
Persuading at me to get a divorce;
    For, says he, if ye dinna,
    Ye're a low stupit ninny,
An' ye'll get nae rest but in the grave.

But he was a lawyer—an' so you see
Ilk thing that he said was a great muckle lee ;
But the very attempt put my wife in a fever,
An' nought but a muckle-wigged doctor could save
    her,
        Wha swore by the rood
        He wad do what he could
    To rescue my spouse frae the grave.

But he was a doctor—an' so you see
My ill-natured Katty began to dee ;
So in a few days she was laid in the mool,
An' I was delivered frae a' my dool :
        So I fand I was right,
        That to do what I might,
    My only relief was the grave.

The Swine.

A SKETCH.

My twa swine on the midden,
Wi' very fat their een are hidden,
Their wames are swell'd beyond dimension,
Their shapes!—ye hae nae comprehension.

Sic a sicht!—their tails sae curly,
Their houghs sae round, their necks sae burly;
In the warld there's naething bigger
Than the tane—except the tither!

Fragments.

THE BARLEY-FEVER.

On the Barley-fever!
The Barley-fever, the Barley-fever!
It sticks like a burr, or a plough in a fur,
    An' it fells a man like a cleaver.
Yer beard turns lang, an' yer head turns bald,
An' yer face grows as white as the lip o' a scald;
Yer tae end is het, an' the tither is cauld,
    Like a rat wi' its tail in a siever.

Oh the Barley-fever!
The Barley-fever, the Barley-fever!
It gars the best soul grow as toom as a bowl,
    An' as flat as the doup o' a weaver.
The Typhus tak's folk that are no very clean,
The Scarlet's content wi' a fat fozy wean;
But the Barley tak's rich, poor, clean, dirty, fat, lean,
    The infidel and the believer.

THE MILLER.

THE Miller's rung did deeds o' weir,
  For mortal fray it aye was ready;
The Miller kent neither sloth nor fear
  When he fought for king or bonnie leddy!
His head was pruif o' stane or steel,
  His skin was teugher than bend-leather;
He could pu' against his ain mill-wheel,
  Or snap in bits his horse's tether.

—

THE FULE'S SANG.

LEDDIES they sing leddies' sangs,
  An' men they sing men's,
An' fules they sing foolish sangs,
  As a' the world kens;
But a' the fule's foolish sangs
  That e'er cam' frae the moon,
Were naething to a sang I heard,
  To a very foolish tune,
    That a fule sang to me.

THE ALEHOUSE.

A' human joys come to an end
　　Some time or ither:
The songsters had nae mair to spend,
　　An' though the weather
Was maist enough to kill a brute,
Auld Luckie cam' an' drave them out.

WOMAN.

Like a clear rippling stream
Glancing in the sunny beam
So artless pure does woman seem—
　　Whistle o'er the lave o't!
She's like (as we in beuks may read)
The daisy blooming on the mead,
A helpless, sweet, bit bonny weed—
　　Whistle o'er the lave o't!

Epigrams.

ON HEARING A LADY PRAISE A CERTAIN REV. DOCTOR'S EYES.

I CANNOT praise the Doctor's eyes,
    I never saw his glance divine;
He always shuts them when he prays,
    And when he preaches he shuts mine.

A' THINGS created have their uses;
    This truth will bear nae doots,
As far as hands to fleas an' louses,
    An' ither bitin' brutes:
I ken the use o' crawlin' clocks,
    An' bugs upon you creepin';
But what's the use o' Barbara Fox?
    By Jingo! that's a deep ane.

ON MISS GRACE C——.

In days of yore the saints oft prayed,
    For grace to keep them from all evil;
Sure sinners now for grace may hope,
    Since Grace is going to the devil.

——— · ——— ——

ON DAVID ——, AN EGOTIST.

A Grecian Sage one day found out
That all he ever knew was nought,
    Which made a wondrous noise;
But greater praise is David's due,
Who found out more than others knew,
    Namely—that he was wise!

'Twixt Joan and Chloe who'll decide
    The precedence in evil?
Fair Chloe could corrupt a saint,
    Joan could corrupt the devil.

Epitaphs.

HERE LIES.

HERE lies, of sense bereft—
 But sense he never had ;
Here lies, by feeling left—
 But that is just as bad ;
Here lies, reduced to dirt—
 That's what he always was ;
Here lies, without a heart—
 He ne'er had one, alas !

Here lies . . . .
 He did so ere he died ;
Then simply to begin,—Here lies—
 But all his life he lied.
Death is a change, they say,—
 Ye powers that rule the sky,
What change is here, I pray ?
 For surely he did die.

AN EPITAPH AND RETROSPECT.

Beneath this rude and little honoured urn
    The bones of one still little loved repose:
Few know or care what cause he had to mourn,
    And fewer still could sorrow for his woes.

Nor cold nor hunger cursed his lowly fate;
    Nor faithlessness of friends, nor scorn of men;
Nor vain ambitious dreams, found false too late;
    Nor rude oppression caused his bosom's pain.

He loved mankind—he still was just and true—
    Still he brought succour to the weak and poor;
He wished to make each mourner glad—but few,
    Few were his means the bleeding soul to cure.

If you have ever grieved, he grieved for you—
    For every woe his sympathy could claim;
He wept for all, while yet his tears could flow—
    Now he is gone!—and who will weep for him?

NOTES

NOTES ON "THE FACULTY ROLL."

Note 1, page 45, line 8.

"*The flocks round Brodie's Stair.*"

Sir James Dalrymple, Viscount Stair, was President of the Court of Session in 1671 and subsequently, and was a chief actor in the Scottish politics of the day. He was the author of 'Stair's Institutions,' a work on the law of Scotland, which was published in 1681, and has always been considered a high authority on the law of Scotland.

An edition of the 'Institutions,' with copious notes, and additions stating the changes which had taken place in the law since Stair's time, was published in 1826-31 by Mr George Brodie, Advocate, who entered the Faculty in the year 1811. It is the work alluded to as 'Brodie's Stair.' Mr Brodie was also author of a 'History of the British Empire from the Accession of Charles I. to the

Restoration,' and held the appointment of Histori-
ographer-Royal of Scotland from 1836 till his
death in 1867.

Note 2, page 45, line 9.

"*Who ruminate on Shaw and Tait.*"

Mr Patrick Shaw was compiler of a series of
Reports of Cases decided in the Court of Session
for a number of years subsequent to 1822, and
his Reports have always been accepted as author-
ities under the name of 'Shaw's Reports.' He
was also Editor of a very useful 'Digest' or
analysis of reported cases, and of an edition of
'Bell's Commentaries.' Mr Shaw entered the
Faculty in the year 1819, and was Sheriff of
Chancery from 1848 to 1869, when he resigned.

The reference to "Tait" applies to a copious
Index of Reported Cases, which was published
in 1823 by Messrs W. & C. Tait, booksellers,
Edinburgh.

Note 3, page 46, line 1.

"*Although our Brough'm you've stolen.*"

Lord Brougham entered the Faculty of Advocates in the year 1800. He did not continue

in practice, having joined the English Bar; and after a most distinguished career, both as a barrister and a politician, he became Lord Chancellor of England in the year 1830.

Note 4, page 46, line 3.

" He may be spared—our hoary Baird."

Mr Thomas Walker Baird entered the Faculty in the year 1793, and was entitled to be called "hoary" when the song was written. He was an eminent Chamber Counsel, and especially conversant with questions of feudal law and conveyancing. He died in 1846.

Note 5, page 46, lines 5 and 7.

" And though you've got some kindly Scotts,

. . . . .

We're the rest, and the best."

The family name of Lord Chancellor Eldon and of his brother Lord Stowell was Scott. Both were members of the English Bar. At the Scotch Bar, at the date of the song, were Mr G. R. Scott, who entered the Faculty in 1786, and Sir Walter Scott, Bart., who entered in the year 1792. Sir

Walter held the offices of Principal Clerk of Session, and Sheriff of Selkirkshire, and is doubtless referred to as "the best." Sir Walter died in 1832. His works are too well known to require any notice here.

Note 6, page 46, line 9.

" *To garrison old Morison.*"

Mr William Maxwell Morison entered the Faculty in the year 1784. He was compiler of a Dictionary of Decisions of the Court of Session, consisting of 40 vols. quarto, and extending from nearly the first institution of the Court. It is a work of standard authority, and is quoted under the name of 'Morison's Dictionary.'

Note 7, page 46, line 12.

" *Our Brown, Reid, White, and Gray.*"

Several gentlemen of the name of Brown were members of the Faculty at the period of the poem. Mr Robert Broun entered in 1780, and was alive in 1832. Mr M. P. Brown entered in 1816; Mr H. H. Broun in 1822; Mr Thomas Broun of Lanfine (a nephew of Lord Jeffrey) in 1825; and Mr James Browne in 1826.

Sir James J. Reid of Mousewald, Dumfriesshire, entered the Faculty in 1827. He was one of the Royal Commissioners on Ecclesiastical Endowments, and afterwards Chief-Justice of the Ionian Islands. The family have been hereditary members of the Bar and the legal profession. Sir James's father entered the Faculty in 1798. Mr J. J. Reid, his eldest son, entered in 1870, and is Queen's Remembrancer in the Scottish Exchequer. Mr R. T. Reid, his second son, is a distinguished Queen's Counsel at the English Bar, and is now M.P. for the Dumfries Burghs.

Mr Alexander White entered the Faculty in 1797. Mr William L. White of Kellerstain entered the Faculty in 1816.

Mr J. H. Gray of Carntyne, a Deputy-Lieutenant of Lanarkshire, entered in 1825.

Note 8, page 46, line 14.

"*You're seen their distant Rae.*"

Sir William Rae, Bart., entered the Faculty in the year 1791. He was Lord Advocate of Scotland under the Administration of Lord Liverpool, and again under the Administrations of the Duke of Wellington and Sir Robert Peel, and M.P. for Buteshire.

Note 9, page 46, line 17.

" And ne'er roam from their Home."

Mr Francis Home, son of Professor Home of Cowdenknowes, entered the Faculty in 1825. He was Sheriff-Substitute of Kinross-shire, and afterwards of Linlithgowshire, which office he held for 41 years. This ancient family were proprietors of Cowdenknowes, on Leader Water, for five or six centuries.

Note 10, page 47, line 1.

" The Lothians, Ross, and Sutherland."

Mr Edward Lothian entered the Faculty in 1815. Mr Alexander Lothian in 1821.

Mr Charles Ross, son of Lord Ankerville, entered in 1789. Mr George Ross, son of Admiral Sir John Lockhart-Ross of Balnagown, entered the Faculty in 1797. He was one of the Judges of the Commissary or Consistorial Court, now abolished.

Mr David Ross entered in 1820.

Mr George Sutherland of Forss entered in 1833.

Note 11, page 47, line 5.

" One foot of Erskine's Institute."

Mr John Erskine of Carnock entered the Faculty in the year 1719. He was Professor of Scots Law in the University of Edinburgh from 1737 to 1765, and was the author of ' Erskine's Principles of the Law of Scotland,' published in 1754, and of ' Erskine's Institute,' published in 1773—works which, like ' Stair's Institutions,' have always been regarded as of the highest authority on Scottish law. Many editions of the ' Institute ' have been published by subsequent editors.

Note 12, page 47, line 8.

" Should never more Shank More."

Mr J. Shank More entered the Faculty in the year 1806. He was editor of editions of ' Stair's Institutions ' and of ' Erskine's Principles,' and was Professor of Scots Law in Edinburgh University.

Note 13, page 47, line 9.

"Our Marshall's Steele, the knaves should feel."

Mr John Marshall entered the Faculty in 1818. He was specially eminent as a Chamber Counsel. He was elected Dean, and was afterwards a Judge of the Court of Session under the title of Lord Currichill.

Mr William Steele entered the Faculty in 1824, and was for many years Sheriff-Substitute of Dumbartonshire.

Note 14, page 47, line 11.

"Have at them with a plump of Spiers."

Mr Graham Speirs entered the Faculty in the year 1820. He was Sheriff of Elgin and Moray, and afterwards of Mid-Lothian, and one of the leaders of the party which ultimately formed the Free Church, and is designated by Lord Cockburn in his 'Journal' as "the Apostolic Spiers."

Note 15, page 47, line 13.

"Let the thieves meet our Neaves."

Mr Charles Neaves entered the Faculty in the year 1822. He was Solicitor-General for Scotland under the Administration of Lord Derby, and was afterwards a Judge of the Court of Session under the title of Lord Neaves. He was a man of great wit and humour, and the author of many exquisite songs, in one of which he happily says of the "Permissive Bill" of the day—

> "Oh ! it's a little simple Bill,
> That seeks to pass *incog.*,
> To *permit* ME—to *prevent* YOU—
> From having a glass of grog."

A small collection of the songs was published by Messrs Blackwood in 1868, under the title of 'Songs and Verses, Social and Scientific, by an old Contributor to Maga.'

After the death of Mr Henry Glassford Bell, the Sheriff of Lanarkshire, there was found among his papers the following graceful tribute to Lord Neaves, which had not been included in any of the Sheriff's published works :—

> "There was a boy, a bright-eyed boy, the dux of all the school,
> Who kept the place at midsummer which he had gained at Yule ;
> Through Horace, Terence, Juvenal, he cantered at his ease
> Nor boggled at the hardest bits of old Thucydides.
> No mathematics daunted him ; he needed small instruction
> To dive at once into the depths of algebra and fluxion.
> There's not a dry eye in the school the day on which he leaves,
> Yet little did the rector know that boy would be Lord Neaves.

There was a lad, an eager lad, who studied day and night,
Whose spirit, through all realms of thought, pursued a
    lofty flight;
Who walked away with every prize in every class at college,
And left unopened not one gate of all the gates of knowledge.
And yet he was no cold recluse, but *débonnaire* and free,
As one who feels that social ties exalt philosophy;
Professors smiling, shake his hand, the Principal believes,
The day may come when that fine lad may live to be Lord
    Neaves.

There was a man, an earnest man, who took to study law,
He waded through old Morison, he swam ahead of Shaw;
He took the marrow out of Stair, the entrails out of Bell,
He sucked the egg of Erskine, and left nothing but the
    shell.
He quoted case and precedent, unravelled every twist,
From darkened legal quiddity he cleared away the mist;
The judges gaze in wonderment, and whisper in their sleeves,
' That man, whene'er the Whigs go out, is sure to be Lord
    Neaves.'

There was a father who had wed a fair and gentle dame,
And more than all his honours prized a husband's, father's,
    name;
Who, as he trod the road of life, through all its weary miles,
Found ever at his own fireside sweet faces and fair smiles.
Ah! better than ambition's fire, or triumph, or success,
Soft eyes that look into our own, loved hands our own that
    press;
'Tis never for himself alone a father toils, achieves,
Tis for the well-known voice that says, ' Papa will be Lord
    Neaves.'

There is a judge whom all the land esteems as wise and
good,
Most fixed in what he deems the right, yet never harsh nor
rude ;
Clear in his office, faithful, just, more pleased to bless than
ban,
And proving that the soundest law comes from the kindliest
man.
For him, the dux of all the school and student ripe, sur-
vives
Youth's freshness, age's wisdom still unite the noblest lives ;
And every compeer lovingly, and with delight receives,
The valued friend, the honoured judge, the unspoilt man—
Lord Neaves."

Note 16, page 47, line 20.

"'Tis the land of Ivory."

Mr James Ivory entered the Faculty in 1816.
He was Solicitor-General for Scotland under the
Administration of Lord Melbourne, and was afterwards a Judge of the Court of Session under the
title of Lord Ivory.

Note 17, page 48, lines 5 and 6.

*"Our Hall is all surrounded
By Forrest, Loch, and Shaw."*

Mr James Hall, son of Sir James Hall, Bart. of
Dunglass, entered the Faculty in the year 1821.

Sir James Forrest of Comiston, Bart., entered the Faculty in 1803, and was afterwards Lord Provost of Edinburgh.

Mr James Loch entered in 1801, and Mr Patrick Shaw in 1819.   Shaw's works have been already noticed.

Note 18, page 48, lines 7 and 8.

"*A Park, such as you never trod,*
A Hill you never saw."

Mr John Park entered the Faculty in 1829. He was the last Advocate of modern days who appeared at the Bar without a wig.

Mr Norman Hill entered in 1802.   He was a very intimate friend of Outram.

Note 19, page 48, lines 9 and 10.

"*We rest among the summer Hay,*
Beside the Gowan fair."

Sir John Hay, Bart. of Park, entered the Faculty in 1821, and was Sheriff-Substitute of Stirling-shire.   Mr John Hay entered in 1811.   Mr John Wilson Hay entered 1826.   Mr William Gowan entered in 1831.

Note 20, page 48, line 15.

" *We gather Wood and Burnett.*"

Mr Alexander Wood entered the Faculty in
1811. He was Dean of Faculty, and was afterwards a Judge of the Court of Session under the
title of Lord Wood.

Mr Arthur Burnett entered the Faculty in 1819,
and was Sheriff-Substitute of Peeblesshire. He
was a descendant of the well-known Lord Mon-
boddo.

Note 21, page 48, line 18.

" *The Wilde is White with snows.*"

Mr J. Wilde entered the Faculty in 1785, and
died in 1840. He was Professor of Civil Law in
Edinburgh University from 1792 till 1800.

Mr William L. White entered in 1816, as already noticed.

Note 22, page 48, line 19.

" *Our Taylor, and our Hozier.*"

Mr Richard Taylor entered the Faculty in 1812.

Mr James Hozier of Mauldslie, a Deputy-Lieutenant of Lanarkshire, entered in 1815.

Note 23, page 48, lines 23 and 24.

" With Thomson's Acts, through Lord Kames' Tracts,
And Fountainhall, and Stair."

Mr Thomas Thomson entered the Faculty in the
year 1793. During the greater part of his life he
was Deputy-Keeper of the National Registers of
Land Rights, &c., and he also did most important
and valuable work in the historical or literary department of the Register House, and in the department of registration of deeds and land rights.
Besides his careful and judicious superintendence,
copious digests and indexes of the various registers
of land rights were prepared by him, which have
proved invaluable as keys to the registers, by
which they were for the first time made really
and easily serviceable for general use. Many
years were devoted by him to this great and most
important work. Amongst other labours of a
historical and literary kind he arranged and published a large folio edition, in eleven volumes, of
the 'Acts of the Scottish Parliament,' with copious
illustrations. Mr Thomson was appointed one of
the Principal Clerks of Session in 1828. He was
President of the Bannatyne Club in succession to
Sir Walter Scott.

Henry Home, afterwards a Judge of the Court of

Session under the title of Lord Kames, was admitted a member of the Faculty in the year 1723. He published various collections of decisions of the Court, and was the author of 'Essays on British Antiquities,' published in 1747; 'Essays on the Statute Law of Scotland,' in 1757; and 'Principles of Equity,' in 1767.

Sir John Lauder of Fountainhall entered the Faculty in the year 1668, and was a Judge of the Court of Session under the title of Lord Fountainhall. He published a collection of decisions from 1678 to 1712, and was the author of various works in history and chronology. An edition of his 'Chronological Notes of Scottish Affairs,' edited by Sir Walter Scott; an edition of his 'Historical Observes of Memorable Occurrents in Church and State,' edited by Mr Adam Urquhart and Mr David Laing; and an edition of his 'Historical Notices of Scottish Affairs,' edited by Mr Laing, were printed by the Bannatyne Club.

Note 24, page 49, line 1.

" *We're three Milnes, and six Millers.*"

Mr G. W. Mylne and Mr David Milne (now Mr David Milne-Home of Milne Graden) entered the Faculty in the year 1826. The latter gentleman did not continue practice at the Bar. He is of distinguished eminence as a geologist and meteorologist, and in science generally. He is President of the Edinburgh Geological Society, and Chairman of the Scottish Meteorological Society.

Mr Nicol Milne of Fauldonside entered the Faculty in 1827, the same year in which Mr Outram entered.

Sir William Miller, Bart., afterwards a distinguished Judge under the title of Lord Glenlee, entered the Faculty in the year 1777, and was on the bench from 1795 till his resignation in 1840. Mr T. H. Miller, son of Mr Patrick Miller of Dalswinton, entered in the year 1802; Mr John Millar of Ballingall in 1806; Mr James Miller in 1819; Mr William Miller in 1823; Mr James Miller, son of Lord Glenlee, in 1825; and Mr John Miller, jun., in 1829.

Note 25, page 49, line 3.

" *We've two Weirs, and a Lister large.*"

Mr Thomas Weir entered the Faculty in the year 1831. Mr William Weir entered in 1827, and became editor of the 'Daily News' (London). Mr John Lister entered in 1832.

Note 26, page 49, line 5.

"A Horsman too, without a horse."

The Right Hon. Edward Horsman, a nephew of the late Lord Stair, entered the Faculty in 1831. He did not continue practice at the Bar, having devoted himself to political life. He was M.P. for Cockermouth, Stroud, and Liskeard in succession, and was for some time a Lord of the Treasury, and was Chief Secretary for Ireland under the Administration of Viscount Palmerston.

Note 27, page 49, line 14.

"Sometimes a joint to Boyle."

The Right Hon. David Boyle entered the Faculty in the year 1793. He was Solicitor-General for Scotland under the second Administration of the Duke of Portland, and M.P. for Ayrshire from 1807 to 1811, and was appointed Lord Justice-Clerk in 1811, and Lord President of the Court of Session in 1841.

Note 28, page 49, line 15.

"But still Cheape's head and Trotters."

Mr Douglas Cheape entered the Faculty in the year 1819. He was Professor of Civil Law in

Edinburgh University. Mr Cheape was a noted humourist, and was the author of many witty and pungent poetical squibs, chiefly political.

"Cheape's head and Trotters" are to be read as "*sheep's* head and *feet*"—a favourite old Scotch dish.

Mr J. P. Trotter entered the Faculty in the year 1826. He was Sheriff-Substitute of Perthshire at Dunblane, and afterwards of Dumfriesshire.

Mr Richard Trotter, a Deputy-Lieutenant of Mid-Lothian, son of General Trotter of Morton Hall, entered the Faculty in 1823.

Note 29, page 50, line 1.

"But for religion!—Clerks, alas!"

Mr John Clerk entered the Faculty in 1785. He was Solicitor-General in 1806, and was raised to the Bench as Lord Eldin in 1823. He was an eminent wit, very cynical and sarcastic, and especially independent. He was a prosy speaker, and on one occasion, when pleading before a judge whose father had been a distinguished member of the Bench under the same judicial title, he was interrupted by a petulant remark that it was impossible to sit all day listening to a reiteration of "also and likewise,"—to which he promptly replied, that his lordship seemed to consider these words synonymous, and added, in his sharpest tones, that they were not so : " Your lordship's father was Lord ——. You're Lord —— *also*, but I doubt if you're *likewise*."

Mr William Clerk entered the Faculty in the year 1792. He was clerk of the Jury Court when it existed separately from the Court of Session.

Note 30, page 50, line 2.

" And Bells we have to spare."

Mr George Joseph Bell entered the Faculty in 1791. He was author of a learned and valuable work on 'The Mercantile Law of Scotland, in relation chiefly to the subject of Bankruptcy,' which was published in 1804, and is usually quoted as 'Bell's Commentaries,' and of other works upon the law of Scotland, which have always been considered of high authority. Mr Bell was appointed Professor of Scots Law in Edinburgh University in 1822, and one of the Principal Clerks of the Court of Session in 1831.

Mr Archibald Bell entered the Faculty in the year 1798, and was appointed Sheriff of Ayrshire in 1815. Mr Robert Bell entered in the year 1804 : he was Procurator for the Church of

Scotland. Mr George Graham Bell of Crurie
entered in the year 1819. Mr J. M. Bell entered
in the year 1825, and was Sheriff of Kincardine-
shire. Mr William Bell entered in 1824. Mr
Henry Glassford Bell entered in the year 1832,
and was for many years Sheriff-Substitute, and
afterwards Sheriff, of Lanarkshire. He was a
very intimate friend of Mr Outram, and edited
the first edition of the 'Lyrics.' He was author
of a Life of Mary Queen of Scots, of a volume
of poetry, and other works.

Note 31, page 50, line 5.

" Our most devout have Dirleton's Doubts."

Sir John Nisbet of Dirleton entered the Faculty
in the year 1633, and was a Judge of the Court
of Session under the title of Lord Dirleton. He
held at the same time the office of Lord Advocate,
a combination which has never occurred since.
He was the author of a work entitled 'Doubts
and Questions in the Law, especially of Scotland.'
It is usually referred to as 'Dirleton's Doubts,' and
was published in 1698, after his death, being
edited by Sir William Hamilton of Whitelaw.

Note 32, page 50, line 9.

" *We've but one Torrie in our ranks.*"

Mr T. J. Torrie entered the Faculty in the year 1830.

Note 33, page 50, line 13.

" *Because we've the Tawse.*"

Mr John Tawse entered the Faculty in the year 1808.

Note 34, page 50, line 23.

" *Though we've got but one Groat.*"

Mr A. G. Groat entered the Faculty in 1834.

Note 35, page 51, lines 3 and 4.

" *Our live stock's scarce, we have but
A solitary Hog.*"

Mr James M. Hog, son of Mr Thomas Hog of Newliston, entered the Faculty in the year 1822.

Note 36, page 51, line 5.

" *One L'Amy on his Trotters stumps.*"

Mr James L'Amy entered the Faculty in the year 1794. He was Vice-Dean of the

Faculty, and for many years Sheriff of Forfar-shire.

Mr Trotter has been already noticed.

Note 37, page 51, line 6.

"Secure from Wolf or dog."

Mr James Wolfe-Murray must be indicated, as there was no gentleman of the name of Wolf in the Faculty. Mr Wolfe-Murray entered in the year 1782, and was afterwards a Judge of the Court of Session under the title of Lord Cringletie. When he was appointed, doubts were expressed by some as to his legal acquirements, and the well-known cynic, John Clerk of Eldin (who is noticed above), expressed his view in these lines :—

> "Necessity an' Cringletie
> Are fitted to a tittle ;
> Necessity has nae law,
> An' Cringletie as little."

The cynic, however, was wrong. Lord Cringletie proved an excellent judge, and on one occasion the House of Lords, on appeal, reversed a decision from which he had differed, and adopted his opinion as the judgment of the House.

NOTES ON "THE MULTIPLEPOINDING."

Note 1, page 57, line 18.

" There the Dean stands profound as the depths of the sea."

The "Dean" is the Dean or Preses of the Faculty of Advocates, who has a position of seniority at the Scotch Bar. The Right Hon. John Hope was Dean at the date of the song. He entered the Faculty in 1816. He was Solicitor-General for Scotland under the Administration of the Earl of Liverpool. He was afterwards a Judge of the Court of Session, and was Lord Justice-Clerk in the Court of Justiciary. He was a grave and powerful pleader.

Note 2, page 57, line 20.

" And Snaigow—as smooth as its surface could be."

Mr James Keay of Snaigow entered the Faculty in 1799. He was a polished and able speaker.

Note 3, page 57, line 21.

"And Rutherfurd—sharp as the rocks on the lee."

The Right Hon. Andrew Rutherfurd entered the Faculty in 1812. He was Solicitor-General for Scotland under the Administration of Viscount Melbourne, and Lord Advocate under the Administrations of Viscount Melbourne and of Lord John Russell, and was M.P. for the Leith Burghs. He was afterwards a Judge of the Court of Session under the title of Lord Rutherfurd.

While Lord Advocate, he was the author of a number of most valuable and carefully framed Acts of Parliament, in regard chiefly to conveyancing, which greatly simplified Scottish deeds, and materially lessened their expense. He was also the author of an Act by which entails were greatly modified. It bears his name, being usually quoted as the "Rutherfurd Act." He was a most accomplished lawyer and powerful pleader, and was equally eminent in literature and science.

Note 4, page 58, line 1.

"And there stands M'Neill, 'with his nostril all wide.'"

The Right Hon. Duncan M'Neill of Colonsay entered the Faculty in the year 1816. He was

Solicitor-General for Scotland under the Administration of the Duke of Wellington and that of Sir Robert Peel, and Lord Advocate under the latter Administration, and was M.P. for Argyleshire. The poor-law of Scotland was reformed and placed on its present footing under his auspices. Subsequently he was a Judge of the Court of Session under the title of Lord Colonsay, and thereafter Lord President of the Court of Session, and Lord Justice-General in the Court of Justiciary. Ultimately he was raised to the peerage, and sat in the House of Lords as Lord Colonsay.

Note 5, page 58, line 4.

" And Cunninghame's there with his papers untied."

Mr John Cunninghame of Duloch entered the Faculty in 1807. He was Solicitor-General for Scotland under Lord Melbourne's Administration, and afterwards a Judge of the Court of Session, under the title of Lord Cunninghame. He was in large practice when at the Bar. It was sometimes thought that occasionally he was not very careful in reading his briefs, to which the "papers untied" seems to allude. But however this may have been, his clients never suffered.   He was a man of much tact and ready resources.

Note 6, page 58, line 10.

"And Peter the Great looks to Adam the Tall."

Mr Patrick (or as he was more usually called, *Peter*) Robertson entered the Faculty in 1815. He was Dean of the Faculty of Advocates, and ultimately a Judge of the Court of Session under the title of Lord Robertson. He was a man of rare wit and humour, and his rich jokes and sayings, which, if collected, would fill a volume, were greatly enhanced by his portly person, and somewhat heavy and stolid-looking countenance, the gravity of which he could preserve while those around him were convulsed with laughter. His appearance is referred to in a short colloquy with Sir Walter Scott, which went the round of the Parliament House in a few minutes. Before the authorship of the Waverley Novels was acknowledged, Sir Walter happened to be in a group round one of the Parliament House fireplaces, and Peter approaching them, hailed him as "Peveril of the Peak" (an allusion to his high forehead and hair). Sir Walter at once replied, to the amusement of the bystanders, "Better

Peveril o' the Peak than Peter wi' the painsh" (paunch).

Mr Douglas Cheape, who was mentioned in the notes of the "Faculty Roll," had a very neat squib upon Mr Robertson. He was a stanch Tory, but it was commonly said that, after the passing of the first Reform Bill, when Lord Grey's Liberal Administration was in office, Peter lost hopes of his party, and offered his services to the Whigs through Lord Brougham, then Lord Chancellor. Mr Cheape embalmed the incident in the following lines, alluding to Mr Robertson's somewhat unusual bulk :—

> " When Brougham by Robertson was told
> That he'd consent a *place* to hold—
> Surveying, with astonished eyes,
> A rat of such enormous size—
> Said Brougham, 'That may be very true;
> But where's the place that could hold *you?*' "

Mr Adam Anderson entered the Faculty in 1818. He was Solicitor-General for Scotland under Sir Robert Peel's second Administration, and was afterwards a Judge of the Court of Session under the title of Lord Anderson. He was very thin and tall, and hence the *sobriquet* of " Adam the Tall."

The experiences and griefs of the various litigants or claimants are graphically given, and made the means of introducing various forms of Scotch procedure in apt and peculiar terms, which, however, are scarcely intelligible to those unacquainted with Scotch procedure and forms. A brief explanation of these terms will show the author's happy play upon the words.

Note 7, page 58, lines 18-21.

"That she had not disponed in liege poustic *was plain,*
For she ne'er went to kirk or to market again—
So maintains her apparent heir, Donald M'Bean."

As the law of Scotland stood when the song was written, any conveyance of real property could be set aside by the heir-at-law (heir-apparent of the song) if, at the time of the execution of the deed, its granter was labouring under the disease of which he died, and did die of that disease, within forty days of its date, without having during that period been either at church, or in a public market, unsupported. The law held that in such circumstances the maker of the deed was not in a fit state to grant it—not being *in legitima potestate*—abbreviated in legal phrase into the *"liege poustie"* of the song.

A suit to set aside such a deed could be prosecuted only by the heir-at-law of the granter, so this plea is put in the mouth of the "heir-apparent" of poor Janet.

Note 8, page 59, lines 6 and 7.

"And what with arrestments, where'er funds could be,
And charges on bill and extracted decree."

"Arrestment," as explained *ante*, p. 52, is an attachment of personal funds and effects. A "charge" is a formal requisition made by an officer of the law, in virtue of a legal warrant, to a debtor, to make payment within a specified time, under the penalty of execution against him and his effects, if payment be not made.

Note 9, page 59, line 21.

" She swears 'tis an action of ' double distress.' "

An action or suit of multiplepoinding falls under the class of actions which are technically called "actions of double distress." "Distress" means the legal distress, or impediment, caused to a party by the use of arrestments in his hands.

The unhappy claimant's experience leads her to

apply the term in a sense more literal than its
technical one.

Note 10, page 60, lines 1-4.

" *The landlord claimed rent—and he'll best tell you
how*
He got into the process by poinding a cow;
His hypothec is quite hypothetical now."

Under the Scotch law until recently, a landlord
had a special and preferable remedy, against a
tenant for payment of rent, by a writ to sequestrate,
or attach and sell, the effects of the tenant upon the
farm.   This remedy was called the landlord's
hypothec.

Note 11, page 60, line 7.

" *The Suspender was bothered to such a degree.*"

A "suspension," as already explained (*ante*, p.
54), is a suit seeking a stay of execution of a
judgment or a "charge."   The party instituting
it is called the "suspender."

An "arrester" is the party enforcing a writ of
arrestment.   A "forthcoming" is a suit which an
arrester institutes to obtain payment or possession

of funds or goods arrested. The arrester is here supposed to be himself in jail, with no means of *forthcoming*, or getting out of it.

Note 12, page 60, line 13.

" One brought a Reduction—but he has retired."

A "reduction," as noticed *ante*, p. 54, is a suit to set aside a deed executed to the prejudice of the party using it.

Note 13, page 60, line 15.

" The Adjudger—as well as the Legal's expired."

An "adjudication" is a suit in which a creditor seeks to have real property "adjudged," or transferred from his debtor to himself; and judgment in the suit transfers the property to the creditor, who is called the adjudger. The property may, however, be redeemed by the debtor, upon making payment of the creditor's claim within the period of ten years, and these ten years are technically termed the "legal" of an adjudication. These years are supposed to have expired, and the creditor himself to have died, during the slow progress of the multiplepoinding.

Note 14, page 60, lines 18-22.

" No more will the poor Heir-Apparent appear—
By way of a seisin they've seized all his gear;
He's absconded — and now his Retour, it is
*   clear,*
Can't be hoped through the Multiplepoinding."

The title of an heir to his ancestor's real estate
was, at the date of the song, completed or established by a writ called a " seisin," under which
he was infeft or seized in the estate.   His
" seisin " was usually preceded by a " service,"
which was a proceeding instituted by a writ from
the Scotch Chancery Office, under which the
claim of the heir was submitted, by a short form
of process, to a jury, by whom he was served or
declared to be the heir, if he proved his propin-
quity.   The verdict of the jury was " retoured " (or
returned) to the Chancery Office, and the writ
issued thereon by that Office declared the verdict
of the jury, and was technically termed a " retour."
The " seisin," as a separate writ, is now abolished,
but the " service " is still in use, in a different
form.

Note 15, page 61, line 3.

*" But the fund, though in medio, has gone to pot
too."*

The *" fund in medio "* is the fund or estate for
which the different claimants have been contending. The protracted endurance of the suit has
exhausted the fund, as well as the claimants.

Note 16, page 61, lines 8-10.

*" And he, whom they call Common Debtor, alone
Has uncommon good luck—he's got off with his
own !"*

The *" common debtor,"* as explained *ante*, p. 53,
is the person for whose funds the claimants have
been contending, and he, being a passive onlooker,
is represented as the only one who has not come
to grief through the multiplepoinding.

NOTES ON
"THE PROCESS OF AUGMENTATION."

Note 1, page 78, line 4.

" Though some may hold their lands cum decimis inclusis."

A title to lands *cum decimis inclusis* (*i.e.*, with teinds included) places the teinds of these lands in a very favourable position, as such lands are exempted from all augmentations of stipend. The following song in Lord Neaves's volume, noticed *ante*, p. 185, refers, in amusing terms, to the position of lands held *" cum decimis inclusis,"* and to a danger which may arise if the terms of the clause are not technically complete. It also refers specially to this song of Outram's, the humour of which Lord Neaves richly relished :—

> " I've often wished it were my fate,
> Enriched by Fortune's bounty,
> To own a little nice Estate
> In some delightful county;

Where I, perhaps, with some applause
   Might cultivate the Muses,
And till my lands, and have a clause
   Cum decimis inclusis.

Wherever no such clause appears,
   You're doomed to much vexation ;
The Minister, each twenty years,
   Pursues his augmentation.
Like any fiend he grabs your teind
   Unless the Court refuses,
And all are sold who do not hold
   Cum decimis inclusis.

That strife to tell, would answer well
   This tune of Maggie Lauder,
When half the Bar are waging war
   About the extra cha'der.
But Outram's wit that scene has hit,
   And all so much amuses,
That I refrain, and turn my strain
   To *decimis inclusis.*

. . . . . .

A friend of mine had such a grant,
   And did not get it *gratis;*
But when produced, 'twas found to want
   The *nunquam separatis.*
An Heritor with such a flaw
   His whole exemption loses,
And might as well possess, in law,
   No *decimis inclusis.*

Then ere you buy, your titles try,
   For fear they're in disorder :
An Old Church feu's the thing for you,
   From some Cistercian Order.

Demand a progress stanch and tight,
   For nothing that excuses,
And see your *nunquam antea*'s right
   As well as your *inclusis*.

Then free from fear and free from strife,
   Your cares and troubles over,
You'll lead a gay and easy life
   Among your corn and clover.
The whole Teind Court you'll make your sport,
   Which else such awe diffuses,
'Augment away,' you'll blithely say,
   'I've *decimis inclusis*.'"

Note 2, page 78, line 18.

"'Tis partly paid in Bear, and partly paid in Barley."

In the scheme of locality, the stipend is fixed or allocated in grain, the value of which, as converted into money by the Clerk of Court in the "Scheme of Locality," is paid to the clergyman.

Note 3, page 79, lines 11-13.

*"A small mortification
Just keeps my wife in clothes."*

In Scottish legal phraseology a "mortification" is the term applied to land, vested in perpetuity in

trustees or otherwise, for payment of the annual
income or produce to such person, or for such
purposes, as may be directed in the deed of mortification. In the city of Aberdeen there is a considerable amount of property so destined which is
under the charge of a civic officer, who is there
styled the *" Master of Mortifications."*

Note 4, page 80, lines 14 and 15.

" The hale o' the teind,
Parsonage and Vicarage."

Parsonage teinds are payable from crops; vicarage, from small articles such as poultry.

Note 5, page 85, lines 1-6.

" The Court . . . thus modify."

The fixing of the stipend is termed its " modification."

Note 6, page 86, lines 13-17.

" The process now must tarry
Till the Junior Ordinary

Proceed to prepare,
With his usual care,
A scheme of locality."

The Court having "modified" or fixed the amount of stipend, remit the case to a single Judge, called the Lord Ordinary, to have the scheme of locality, apportioning the amount payable by each heritor, prepared.

Note 7, page 89, line 9.

" My Manse requires repairs."

The minister, being indignant at the result of the augmentation, seeks consolation in devising a new source of vexation, by procedure in the Teind Court, for the repair and enlargement of his "manse" or dwelling-house and offices, which the heritors of the parish are bound to maintain.

NOTES ON "THE LAW OF MARRIAGE."

Note 1, page 93, lines 5 and 6.

" No matter!—I espoused a maid of twenty
By promise, and a process subsequente."

By the law of Scotland marriage may, in certain circumstances, be validly constituted by an interchange of promise of marriage between the parties.

Note 2, page 94, lines 10 and 11.

" The feudalist may learnedly explain
When its avail is single and when double."

Under the old Scotch feudal law a proprietor of land was liable to pay to his feudal superior, or over-lord, a "casualty" or fine on various events occurring, and among others upon his being married. It was termed "the avail of marriage," and varied in amount according to circumstances —hence the legal term "single or double avail."

Note 3, page 95, line 2.

" The Lords dispensed, they told me, with the habit."

This refers to the suit of *cessio bonorum*. By the old law of Scotland a bankrupt was bound to wear a particular description of dress or habit. By the judgment in the suit of *cessio bonorum*, the Court "dispensed with," or relieved, the debtor, from the obligation to wear that dress, which was technically styled in the judgment as "dispensing with the habit."

Note 4, page 95, line 13.

" I then attempted Vitious Intromission."

One who takes possession of the property of a deceased relative without the legal authority of "confirmation" or probate, is called a "vitious intromitter," and his dealings with it "vitious intromission." In the line, theft, of course, is implied.

Note 5, page 95, lines 17-20.

" No letters came to me of Open Doors ;
Criminal letters, though, came postage free.

The air I breathed just added to my cares,
Reminding me of coming Justice Ayres."

Letters of open doors form a writ, or portion of
a writ, authorising prison doors to be opened—
or in other words, the liberation of a prisoner.
"Criminal letters" are one form of the indictment
or charge under which an accused party is brought
to trial. "Justice Ayres" are meetings of the
Court of Justiciary for the trial of prisoners.

NOTES ON "IS THE HOUSE WARM YET?"

Note 1, page 157, line 1.

"When Bell begins to falter in his boisterous career."

Mr Henry Glassford Bell, noticed previously under "The Faculty Roll."

Note 2, page 157, line 2.

"And Mackenzie's merry voice begins to sound a little queer."

Thomas Mackenzie, Esq., advocate, who was Solicitor-General for Scotland under Lord Aberdeen's Administration, afterwards on the Scotch bench as Lord Mackenzie. He was a contemporary of Outram at the Bar, and an early and attached friend, and of a very kind and genial temperament, with no small spice of quiet humour.

Note 3, page 157, line 4.

"And Hill's becoming tuneless."

Mr D. O. Hill, of the Royal Scottish Academy. He held a high place as an artist. One of his pictures is a view of Edinburgh from the Castle, which was engraved, and is esteemed as one of the best views of the city. He was a very sweet singer, and had a large repertory of curious old songs. He and Outram were most attached friends.

Note 4, page 157, line 8.

" When Rhind begins, with husky throat, to over-
ture the chair."

Macduff Rhind, Esq., advocate, for many years Sheriff - Substitute of Wigtownshire. He was a contemporary of Outram at the Bar, and a very intimate friend.

Note 5, page 157, line 10.

" And the joyous-hearted Crutherland seems quite
o'ercome wi' care."

John Smith of Crutherland, LL.D. of Glasgow University. He was editor of many of the pub-

lications of the Maitland Club, and intimately
acquainted with all the literary men of the day.

Note 6, page 157, line 12.

" *And Ellis seems at sea.*"

Mr William M. Ellis, advocate, a contemporary
at the Bar, and intimate friend of Outram, and a
keen yachtsman.

Note 7, page 157, line 16.

" *When Macnee confuses Archie wi' the little
Paisley boy.*"

Sir Daniel Macnee, afterwards President of
the Royal Scottish Academy, a well-known and
highly esteemed artist, and most lovable man. At
the time the song was written, and until he became President of the Academy, he was resident
in Glasgow, and filled a high place in Glasgow
society. He had a marvellous collection of original stories, in which he delineated character
with infinite effect — touching the peculiarities
of the Highlander, and of the denizens of Glasgow, Paisley, and Greenock, with most amusing
faithfulness and grace. In the song he is repre-

sented as making a muddle of two of his stories. He was a very intimate and attached friend of Outram.

Note 8, page 157, line 18.

"And Dunbar's tongue is motionless by sheer excess of joy."

Mr William Dunbar, advocate, noticed in the " Faculty Roll."

Note 9, page 157, line 20.

" And Spens calls it doubly hazardous."

Mr William Spens became manager of the Scottish Amicable Insurance Company in 1839. He was a Fellow of the Faculty of Actuaries in Scotland, and of the Institute of Actuaries of Great Britain and Ireland.

Note 10, page 158, line 1.

" When Salmond breaks his glass and seeks to justify the deed."

Mr George Salmond, Procurator-Fiscal for the county of Lanark. In the Glasgow Directory of

1855-56, he is called Commissary and Admiral of Lanarkshire.

Note 11, page 158, line 3.

"And the Doctor frae Gartnavel tries to stand upon his head."

Dr William Hutchison, resident physician of the Gartnavel Lunatic Asylum from its opening in 1842 to 1850.

NOTES ON "AN APPEAL FROM THE SHERIFF."

Mr Henry Cockburn, the author of the "Epigram," entered the Faculty in the year 1800. He was Solicitor-General under the administration of Earl Grey, and was afterwards a Judge of the Court of Session under the title of Lord Cockburn.

During the greater part of his life Henry Cockburn kept a journal, which (or copious extracts from it) was published after his death. It is highly interesting and amusing, and contains at the same time much valuable information upon most of the public questions of the period.

Cockburn was in his day the most eloquent and persuasive orator at the Scottish Bar. With his impressive oratory, his expressive face and fine eye, his mellow voice, and his pure and homely Scottish dialect, he was almost irresistible with a jury, or in the General Assembly of the Church, in which he was often engaged as counsel.

On the trial of the infamous Burke and his wife, in 1829, for numerous murders of unfortunate creatures whom they lured into their den and murdered, and whose bodies they sold, for dissection, he acted as counsel for the woman. The trial lasted till five in the morning of the second day, and after sixteen or seventeen hours' previous exertion, he addressed the jury, in one of the most impassioned and powerful speeches he ever delivered. He spoke for an hour, and literally held the jury and the audience spell-bound. His chief ·aim was to break down the evidence of Hare, and his wife, who were *socii crimines*, and had been admitted by the Crown as approvers. While the miserable woman was giving her evidence, she had a child in her arms, who continued to scream almost incessantly. After drawing, in scathing and terrible words, a picture of her and Hare's atrocities, whom he represented as the real criminals, he ascribed the screaming of the child to terror, "as if it had felt the fingers of the murderous hag clutching its little innocent throat." His peroration, delivered with a glistening eye, in tones of the utmost solemnity and pathos, put it to the jury that there was no real evidence except that of the approvers, and that if they found the accused guilty upon such evidence as that of the two

Hares, these (pointing with a tremulous hand to the accused) " will be murdered, and these " (pointing to the jury) " will be perjured." Horrified as all those in Court had been at the fearful atrocities disclosed on the trial, there was, when he sat down, a universal hum of sympathy from the large audience. His speech saved the woman's life; for, while the jury found the man guilty, their verdict in the case of the woman was " not proven."

For racy wit and humour Cockburn was equally distinguished as he was for eloquence. Like Peter Robertson's, his jokes and quips would fill a volume. As examples, the following may be given :—

On one occasion he was engaged in a case in which some miscreant had ill-used and maimed a farmer's cattle by cutting off their tails. At the conclusion of a consultation, at which the farmer was present, some conversation took place as to disposing of the animals. Turning to him, Cockburn said the cattle might now be sold, but that he must be content to sell them wholesale, because he could not *retail* them.

On another occasion he was counsel for a man accused of a capital crime, for which, if found guilty, the punishment was death. The evidence was quite conclusive as to the man's guilt. When the jury had retired to consider their verdict, his client roundly taxed him with not having done him justice in the defence. He bore the fellow's insolence for some time, but at last he gave him the pithy reply—"Keep your mind easy, my worthy friend, you'll get *parfait justice* about this time six weeks"—six weeks being then the period allowed to elapse between a sentence of death and its execution.

GLOSSARY.

Action—a suit in court.
Advocate (to)—to appeal from inferior Court to Court of Session.
Ae—one.
Afore—before.
Ailin'—ailing, ill.
Ain own.
Ait—oat.
Allenarlie—only.
Amna am not.
Ance—once.
Ane—one.
Anent—concerning.
Anither—another.
Appeteet - appetite.
Auld old.
Auld Nick - Satan.
Ava at all, at any time.
Awa'—away.
Ayont beyond.

Ba' ball.
Backbane backbone.
Backspang a trick or quirk, or return to previous condition.
Baith - both.
Band bond, agreement.
Bane—bone.
Bangs strikes.
Bannock—a thick cake toasted on a girdle.
Barkit—barked.

Barley-fever—fever from intoxication, *delirium tremens*.
Bashed—crushed, bruised.
Bedrizzled—sprinkled, wetted.
Begunk—deceive, balk.
Behuved—behoved.
Beil—a bill or account.
Belanged—belonged.
Bellin'- the rising of air-bells in water.
Ben ta house—the inner room of a cottage.
Bend - leather — thick sole-leather.
Bend the bicker — put round the glass.
Beuks books.
Bit part, portion.
Blackmail - a contribution paid to freebooters for exemption.
Blade a reckless young fellow.
Bleerit bleared.
Bluid blood.
Blythe happy, merry.
Boddle half-farthing.
Body a small person.
Bonny pretty.
Boo bow.
Bouse a drinking bout.
Brae—hillock.
Brak broke.
Braw good, full ; also well-dressed.

Breeks—trousers.
Bricht—bright.
Brochan—oatmeal boiled to consistency of gruel.
Brocht—brought.
Broo—brow.
Broozled—broken, bruised.
Buik—book.
Buirdly—strong, powerful.
Burr—the head of a thistle or prickly plant.

Ca'—call.
Canna—cannot.
Cannie — quiet, peaceable, careful.
Canty—lively, cheerful.
Caption—a writ to apprehend.
Caredna—cared not.
Carlings—broiled peas.
Cassin—revoking, repealing.
Cast—lot, fate, rejected.
Cauld—cold.
Causey—pavement.
Chafts—cheeks.
Chaps — fellows, acquaintances.
Charged—served with a warrant for execution.
Chaws—chews.
Chield—lad, young fellow.
Chow— chew.
Claes—clothes.
Claw—fingers, hand; also to scratch.
Clout — a noisy fall; also a cloth.
Clytes—tumbles, falls.
Coorse — coarse.
Corkscrewity—twisted like a corkscrew.
Cosh—snug, comfortable.
Cot tamn—a Highland oath.
Couldna—could not.
Coups—overturns.
Cozier — warmer, more comfortable.
Cracks her crack — tells her story.

Craigs—throats; also rocks.
Crined awa' — shrunk, shrivelled.
Crookit—crooked.
Croon—to sing in a low tone.
Crouse—brisk, bold.
Crowdie—posset, meal soaked in cold water.
Cuddie-heel — iron heel on shoe.
Cuist up—cast up.
Custock—the core of cabbage, or cabbage-stalk.

Dab—an expert.
Daddie—father.
Daised—stupid, perplexed.
Dauds—strikes.
Daur—dare.
Debitorum—debtors.
Decerns—gives judgment or decreet.
Dee'd—died.
Deleerit—delirious.
Delete—obliterated.
Delved—dug.
Devallin' — ceasing, intermitting.
Dicht—wipe, to clean.
Didna—did not.
Diligence — execution on a judgment of a court.
Dings—thumps, strikes.
Dinna ye—don't you.
Disna does not.
Disponed — conveyed, made over.
Division — the two Inner Chambers of the Court of Session are called "Divisions."
Dizzen—dozen.
Doited—stupid, imbecile.
Dominorum — the Lords of Session.
Donnard—stupid, perplexed.
Dool—grief, sorrow.
Doots—doubts.
Dottrified—become imbecile.
Doun—down.

Douncome—overthrow, fall.
Doup—the sitting part.
Dour—hard, severe, stubborn.
Drammock — meal and water mixed raw, or boiled to pulp.
Drucken—drunken.
Dubs—pools of water.
Dulefu'—doleful.
Dwam—a fit or faint.

Ee—eye.
Een—eyes
E'en now at present.
Eneugh—enough.
Evendown entire, complete.
Exiguity—a scarecrow.

Fa'—fall.
Facility—state of being easily imposed on.
Fadge—barley-meal bannock or loaf.
Failin'—failing in health; also bankruptcy.
Fa'in'—falling.
Fand found.
Farder—further.
Farle—cake.
Fashin' troubling.
Fause false.
Fecht fight.
Fell—earnest, strong.
Fell (to) to kill.
Fend—live, exist.
Fient nothing, never.
Fin - hand or arm.
Fit foot; also habit or custom; also its natural meaning.
Forbye besides.
Forebears—ancestors.
Foregae dispense with.
Forenent— opposite.
Forgather — meet, fall in with.
Forgie forgive.
Forpit—a measure of capacity.
Fou—tipsy.

Fozy—soft, dull.
Frae from.
Fraise—complaint, a cajoling discourse.
Frisky—joyous, playful.
Fu'—full; also tipsy.
Fule—fool.
Fur—furrow.
Fusionless — useless, void of spirit and energy.

Gadgers—officers of revenue.
Gaed—went.
Galore—in profusion, in great plenty.
Gane—gone.
Gang—go.
Gar—cause, make.
Gaun going.
Gear money.
Ghaist- ghost.
Gied—gave.
Gien - given.
Gin—if.
Gleg—sharp, active, lively.
Glow'rin'—staring.
Gotten - got.
Gowan daisy.
Gowd gold.
Grane groan.
Grannie grandmother.
Greet cry, weep.
Growin' growing.
Grund ground, bottom.
Grunts groans, growls.
Gude)
Guid) good.
Gudeman father, head of family.
Guid gangin' good going.
Guidin' guiding.
Gumption sense, cleverness.
Guse goose.

Ha' hall.
Haddie haddock.
Hae have.
Haffits the sides of the head, the temples.

Haidin', haddin', baudin' —holding.

Haill—whole.

Hained—saved.

Halden—held.

Hame—home.

Hams—limbs, calves of leg.

Hash—a sloven; also to abuse or maltreat, or make a muddle; also a stew of butcher-meat cut small.

Hass or hause—throat.

Haud—have, hold.

Haunds—hands.

Helpit—helped.

Het—hot.

Hide—skin.

Hoast—cold, cough.

Houghs — upper limbs, quarters.

Houp—hope.

Howdie—midwife.

Hurkles—crouches.

Ilk Ilka —each.

Ingan—onion.

Ingle-side—fireside.

Ither—other.

Jaud — a term of contempt applied to a woman.

Jorum —a bowl of punch.

Kail—broth, soup.

Kail-pat—broth-pot.

Kaim—comb.

Kebbuck—cheese.

Keepit—kept.

Ken—know.

Ken'd Kent —knew.

Kink—cough.

Kintra—country.

Kirk—church.

Kittle—deadly, difficult; also to tickle.

Knir—a knot in wood.

Knowe—a grassy hillock.

Kye- kine.

Laird—landed proprietor.

Laith—loath.

Lane (his)—alone.

Lang—long.

Lauchin'—laughing.

Lave—remainder.

Lea—farm.

Leal-hearted—true-hearted.

Lear—learning.

Leddy—lady.

Lee—lie.

Len'—loan.

Licht—light.

Lick—thrash; also to lap.

Licking—thrashing; also lapping.

Liket—liked.

Limmer—an opprobrious term showing displeasure; a worthless woman.

Lo'ed—loved.

Loof—hand.

Lookit—looked.

Loon—a shrewd or sly man.

Lounders — thrashings, severe blows.

Loup—leap.

Lowse—loose.

Luckie—a woman, mistress of a house.

Luckpenny—a small part of a price returned to a purchaser for luck.

Lug—ear.

Ma'—may.

Mailin—farm.

Mair—more.

Mak's—makes.

'Mang--amongst.

Manier—manner.

Maun—must.

Mawn—mown.

Meikle—much.

Merk—a piece of Scots money now disused, equal to 1s. 8d. sterling.

Mind—remember.

Mither—mother.

Mool—mould, turf.
Muckle—large, much.
Munches—masticates with difficulty.

Nae—no.
Naething—nothing.
Neb—nose.
Needit—required.
Neist—next.
Neives—hands, fists.
Never devallin'—unceasing.
Nick—cut, break.
Ninny—a nincompoop.
Nip—a small portion.
Nowt—oxen.

Ony—any.
Ower—over.
Owsen—oxen.

Pad—bad.
Paik—a stroke or blow.
Pangin'—cramming.
Pap—gentle stroke.
Paraphernal — a lady's personal dress or ornaments.
Pargain—bargain.
Partan—crab.
Peholden - beholden.
Pickle - small portion.
Pit - put; also its natural meaning.
Pla'—play.
Pleasour—pleasure.
Pleugh—plough.
Plisky plight.
Podley—a small sea-fish.
Poo—bow.
Pookin' - pulling gently.
Poot put.
Pouch pocket.
Powsowdie—sheephead-broth.
Preen—pin.
Process—a legal suit.
Pruif - proof, evidence; also impervious to.
Pruive prove.
Puddin'—pudding.

Puddock—frog.
Puir—poor.
Puirly—poorly.
Pund—pound.
Pu's—pulls.
Pushion—poison.

Queer—strange.

Rantin'—excited, boisterous.
Reamin'—creaming.
Red—rid.
Richt—right.
Rifart—raddish.
Riggin', roof of a cottage.
Rinnin'—running.
Rins—runs.
Riskie—risk.
Rizzard— sun-dried.
Roose—rouse.
Roun'—round.
Rout—cry out.
Rung—cudgel.
Runt — a decayed cabbage-stalk ; also an opprobrious term for an old woman.

Sac—so.
Sair—sore.
Sall—shall.
Sang—song.
Sark shirt, shift.
Saumon—salmon.
Sawted—salted.
Saxty—sixty.
Scadlips—broth containing a little barley.
Scald scold.
Scate-rumples—a portion of a skate.
Scunner—disgust, loathing.
Seisin writ of infeftment in land.
Sell't—sold.
Shae—shoe.
Shaw—show.
Shirra sheriff.
Shool - shovel.
Shoon—shoes.

Shouther - blade — shoulder - blade.

Sic }
Siccan } —such.

Sicht—sight.
Siclike—suchlike.
Siever—drain.
Siller—money.
Skink — soup made of beef-shin much boiled.
Skreighed—screamed, bawled.
Sma'—small.
Sneeshin'—snuff.
Snook'd out—held out, prying or smelling around like a dog.
Snout—nose.
Sookin'—sucking.
Sortin'—tuning; also arranging.
Sough—rumour.
Soun'—sound.
Souple—supple.
Southron—English.
Spak'—spoke.
Speer—inquire.
Spunkie—lively.
Stamack—stomach.
Stane—stone.
Staps—steps.
Steek—shut.
Steer—stir, move.
Sticks out—projects.
Stieve—stiff, strong.
Stour—dust driven by wind.
Stove—stewed.
Stown—stolen.
Stumps about—walks heavily or slowly.
Stupit—stupid.
Submission—arbitration.
Subscrieve—subscribe.
Suld—should.
Sune—soon.
Suppin'—supping.
Swirl—whirl.
Syboe—a young onion with its green tail.
Syne—then.

Ta—the.
Tae—too.
Tae end—the one end.
Taeds—toads.
Taen—taken.
Tane—the one.
Tans—toasts, gets browned.
Tap—top.
Tennity—thinness, leanness.
Terrorem—victim of terror.
Tested—attested by witnesses.
Teugh—tough.
Thegither—together.
Thocht—thought.
Thole—bear, endure.
Threeps—insists, argues.
Timmer—wood, hard.
Tipp't aff—drank off.
Tither—the other.
Toddled—walked totteringly like a child.
Toom—empty.
Toon—town.
Toucher—tougher.
Trig—trim.
Twa—two.
Tyke—dog.

Unco—sad, very.
Unkenn'd — unknown, unknowable.
Usquebaugh—whisky.

Viduity—widowhood.
Vivers—victuals, meats, sustenance.

Wa'—wall.
Wad—would.
Wadna—would not.
Wae—sad, woe.
Waesome—woesome.
Wald—would.
Walth—wealth.
Wame—belly.
Wanchancie—unlucky, unfortunate.
Wares—spends.
Wark—work.

Washin'—washing.
Wasna—was not.
Waur aff—worse off, ill.
Weans—children.
Wee—small.
Weel—well.
Weir—war, fights.
Werena—were not.
Whar—where.
Whilk—which.
Whillywha—coax, impose upon.
Whomelled—tumbled, turned over.
Wi'—with.

Wiuna—will not.
Winsome — lovely, captivating, cheery.
Wizened—shrivelled, dried up, wasted.
Wrack—wreck.
Wrunkled—wrinkled.

Yer—your.
Yerked his head—cudgelled or ransacked his brain.
Yestreen—last night.
Yill—ale.
Youdith—youth.
Yule—Christmas.

www.ingramcontent.com/pod-product-compliance
Lightning Source LLC
Chambersburg PA
CBHW020100030726
47498CB00006B/1876